THE AMBIGUITY OF MURDER

When the body of retired Bolivian diplomat Guido Zavala is found floating in his swimming pool, Inspector Alvarez finds that the evidence might point to foul play and – reluctantly – begins to look for suspects.

As he slowly uncovers Zavala's past, he learns there are those who have good cause to have disliked the man: Jerome Robertson, whose beautiful and much younger wife has been conducting a secret affair with him; Santiago Pons, a builder, whose heavy gambling losses have placed him at the other's financial mercy; Bailey, an honourable man, who suffered in the past because of him.

During his investigations, Alvarez receives threatening phone calls which make it all too clear that his life is in danger. Panicking, he appeals to Superior Chief Salas for help, but this is denied in the name of proud logic. It is left to his irrepressible Cousin Dolores, certain no man is capable of managing to do anything successfully, to take matters into her own hands . . .

A delightful and witty mystery featuring Roderic Jeffries's much-loved Inspector Alvarez.

THE AMBIGUITY
OF MURDER

AN INSPECTOR ALVAREZ NOVEL

Roderic Jeffries

HarperCollins*Publishers*

This novel is entirely a work of fiction. The names, characters and incidents portrayed in it are the work of the author's imagination. Any resemblance to actual persons, living or dead, events or localities is entirely coincidental.

Collins Crime
An imprint of HarperCollins*Publishers*
77–85 Fulham Palace Road, London W6 8JB

The Collins Crime website address is:
www.collins-crime.com

First published in Great Britain
in 1999 by Collins Crime

1 3 5 7 9 10 8 6 4 2

A catalogue record for this book
is available from the British Library

ISBN 0 00 232687 6

Typeset in Meridien and Bodoni
by Palimpsest Book Production Limited,
Polmont, Stirlingshire

Printed and bound in Great Britain by
Clays Ltd, St Ives plc

CHAPTER 1

In the public car park, Fenella sat behind the wheel of the Rover and willed the minutes away. Every visiting day she had promised herself she would not arrive early and have to sit and wait, wishing, like a child, that the impossible would happen; every visiting day, she had failed her promise. Now she was equally early and time had slowed almost to a halt . . .

A man turned the corner of the nearest building and her heart shouted Harry, before her eyes, guided by common sense, identified him from his clothes as a warder. He bore hardly any resemblance to Harry . . . If you don't turn up soon, my love, I'll be confusing you with little green men from Mars . . .

Two men appeared down the right-hand path beyond the outside building, and while one of them was another warder, the second was Harry. But they came to a stop and talked . . . Why the hell aren't you rushing to me? . . . He never allowed his emotions free rein; had not, even when he knew his world was about to collapse about him . . . Harry, if you don't rush now, I'll scream blue, bloody murder . . .

He finally shook hands with the warder, walked towards the Rover, the collar of his overcoat turned up against the wind which blew out of a sullen sky that promised yet more rain in what was proving to be a real Filldyke February . . . You're even thinner; you're looking haggard. You need good food and love beyond satiation . . .

She opened the door and stepped out of the car. Unlike him, she had no intention of restraining her emotions and she ran forward. As she wrapped herself around him, she could hear a Hollywood choir.

*　　*　　*

1

As they drove along the country lane, bordered by thorn hedges and an occasional tree, she sat sideways in the passenger seat so that she could stare directly at him. He had a high forehead. Soon after meeting him, she'd joked that this denoted great intelligence. The first whisper of baldness had been his reply. He might be of the present, but he belonged to the past, to the age when a man pursued modesty. His eyes were an ever-changing blue. He claimed that that was impossible, but it was true. His nose was Roman – brave Horatius, the Captain of the Gate, must have sported such a nose. His lips were full and . . .

'You've become very silent,' he said.

. . . And shaped for love. She briefly put her hand on his left thigh. 'If I tell you what I'm thinking, you'll cringe at the woman's gush.'

He laughed.

'Do you know what you do to me when you laugh like that?'

'Tell me.'

'You make me want to throw myself into your arms.'

'Then in the name of road safety, I won't laugh again until we arrive.' He braked for a corner. 'Fen.'

'What?'

Once round the corner, he accelerated. 'Are you sure it's sensible to go to your place?'

'Where else can you suggest?'

'Since my place went to Anne in the divorce settlement, it'll have to be a hotel.'

'We celebrate in some coldly anonymous room after all you've been through?'

'James is hardly going to welcome my appearance. Not after all that's happened.'

She settled back in the seat and stared through the windscreen, her expression strained.

'I'd hate to cause any more trouble.'

'He died eight months ago.'

In his surprise, he let the car drift on the low grass bank and the near-side front wheel briefly bumped along its uneven surface. As he hurriedly steered back on to the road, he said: 'Why on earth didn't you tell me?'

'Where was the point? There was nothing you could do. And if you'd known, it would only have made things worse for you.'

'But . . .' He became silent. What she said was true. All he could have offered would have been words and they seldom assuaged pain. 'Was it . . . Was he . . .'

'The past is the past. We've each other and that's all that matters.'

Could one ever dismiss the past? he wondered.

Brakebourne House stood in the centre of a row of Edwardian houses. Three floors high and relatively narrow, it lacked good proportions and its appearance was only redeemed by the odd-shaped, stone-bordered windows, which provided a certain quirkiness.

They lay in bed in the main bedroom; he on his back, she on her side and pressed against him.

'Well?' she said.

'The score out of ten? Eleven.'

'Thank goodness it wasn't a mere nine.' She moved until she could rest her breasts on his chest and kiss him. 'When I allowed myself to dream, we made such imaginative love that I drove your pain away.'

'You've exceeded all expectations.'

The rain increased and the wind swept it against the window with a drumming sound. He said, his voice distant: 'When it rained as hard as this, the roof leaked and water dripped with irritating monotony on to the floor between my bed and the next one. Each time it happened, I reported it and they said repairs would be carried out, but they never were. I reckon the secret of good prison management is to make certain that nothing changes.'

'Was it very terrible? Or don't you want to talk about it?'

Several seconds passed before he said: 'There's the old chestnut that if you've suffered public school, prison's a piece of cake. There's a little truth in that. But when one's an adult, it's difficult to accept stupidity in the name of discipline . . . Still, it was a loose regime compared to a closed prison and the only real problem was successfully defending one's virtue.'

'What were the staff like?'

'The mixture one meets anywhere; some good, some bad, some indifferent. I was lucky. One of the screws had a secret liking for romantic poetry.'

'Why secret?'

'In such a regime, that sort of passion is regarded with the deepest suspicion.'

'How did you discover he liked it?'

'Shortly after I arrived, he told me to weed one of the flower beds. Being facetious, to try to keep my spirits above freezing, I said, "A host, of golden daffodils; beside the mess, beneath the trees." Instead of bawling me out for insolence, he assumed I was a Wordsworth fanatic and had me posted as assistant librarian. From time to time he discussed poetry with me and since he knew far more than I could remember, I had to do a lot of surreptitious revision. It paid off. He was usually ready to give a spot of advice and more than once enabled me to avoid trouble.'

'What sort of trouble?'

'As it's an open prison, in theory all the inmates are non-violent, but people's concepts of what constitutes violence varies. For some, knocking hell out of someone is no more than horseplay and I'd probably have been well on the receiving end because of my obvious background if he hadn't advised me how to act when things started looking dicey.'

'You'd have been badly hurt?'

'More than likely.'

'Bastards!'

'On the face of things, yes. But most of them have led rough lives so their values are completely different.'

'I meant the lawyers.'

'You can't blame them . . .'

'I can! Why do you have to be so bloody forgiving?'

'It's supposed to get you to heaven quicker.'

'You're hiding the truth, aren't you? You're being facetious to cover the fact that every moment was pure hell, made far worse because you weren't guilty.'

'That certainly didn't help.'

She kissed him with passion, trying to drive past hurt from his mind and fear of the past from her own. In the nature of things, she succeeded in doing both for a while.

Later, when the rain had eased and objects seen through the window were distorted rather than a meaningless blur, he said: 'Did James ever . . .' He came to a stop.

'Understand?'

'I suppose that's as good a word as any.'

'He couldn't.'

'He still thought it was because of his illness, not despite it?'

'I tried and tried to make him understand . . . For God's sake, why do I keep on using that word when it's meaningless since I can't understand myself even. How did it happen? I've always considered myself loyal. But we're asked to a party, James isn't up to it, but persuades me to go because he says I must have a break from illness; I'm standing by the fireplace thinking how odd it is to see people able to lead normal lives and you're introduced . . . And I throw loyalty out of the window!'

'Sometimes, one just isn't in control of one's own life, however hard one tries to be.'

'That's merely excusing weakness.'

'Perhaps. It's also true.'

'If Anne hadn't been having another affair, would you have been so eager?'

'It was nothing to do with attitudes, all to do with phero-mones. They're irresistible. Female moths release them and in no time at all they're surrounded by ardent males.'

'You make it sound as if I hadn't bathed properly.'

'I'm saying that we couldn't have stopped its happening.'

'Not even if we'd known the pain it would cause?'

'I said, they're irresistible.'

'That's a weasel.'

'Sometimes it helps one to see the truth to weasel.'

5

They were silent for a while.

'Don't you think we ought to get up?' she finally asked.

'Why?'

'I'm sure you were brought up to believe it to be decadent to be in bed during the day unless one's ill.'

'Since the only decadence available to me until now has not been to my taste, I say, decade on.'

CHAPTER 2

The sky was cloudless, the sun hot. Orange and lemon trees were in fruit and blossom, fig trees were showing green tips; tomato and sweet pepper plants were already making good growth; the first strawberries were in the shops. Spring had come early to the island.

Karen collected up the shopping bag and her handbag from the passenger seat, opened the driver's door and stepped out of the car. Emilio stood upright in the middle of the nearest flower bed.

'Good morning, señora,' he said.

She liked to practise her Spanish. 'It's a nice day.'

'Now, it is perfect!'

Because of the generosity of so many tourists, every Mallorquin male in the prime of his life imagined himself Don Juan; she didn't doubt that the slightest hint of encouragement on her part would have him breathing heavily as he undressed her with greater skill than he gardened – he found difficulty in distinguishing flower from weed. She smiled a neutral smile, made her way across to the front door, certain that he was appreciating the rhythm of her taut buttocks. She unlocked the door and went into the hall. 'It's me.'

'I'm in here,' Robertson called out.

'Be with you in a second, darling.' She carried the shopping bag into the kitchen, emptied it and put the perishable items in the refrigerator. About to leave, she remembered the two letters she'd collected from the post office and brought them from her handbag.

He was sitting on the settee, watching a soap opera on the television. 'How are you now?' she asked, sounding concerned.

'No better. Worse.' He did not look away from the screen.

7

'It feels like I'm being sawn in half. It's appendicitis, whatever that useless doctor said.'

'But you had your appendix out when you were a boy.'

'They must have left part of it in.'

He'd suggested that – through her, since he took pride in speaking no Spanish – to the doctor. The doctor did not speak any English, so she'd been able to mistranslate his curtly contemptuous reply. 'Have you taken the pills he gave you?'

'No.'

'For goodness sake, why not?'

'They're probably nothing but chalk.'

She gave up. 'There are two letters for you.'

The programme ended and the advertisements began. He used the remote control to switch off the set.

She handed him the letters. He opened the first one and brought out a single sheet of paper. 'What's the use of sending me this?' he demanded angrily.

'What is it?'

'That's just the point. It's in Spanish. Why?'

Because they were living in Spain. When he became annoyed, which was frequently, she mentally compared him to a bedraggled, aging bantam cock. The hairs in his nose needed cutting and his moustache a good wipe. Not Adonis's younger brother. One of the sad facts of life was that so few men had fat bank accounts before they had fat bellies. 'Shall I have a look?' He held out the letter and she took it. After a moment, she said: 'It's in Mallorquin, not Spanish, so I can't be certain, but it looks as if the town hall's putting up the catastral value of this place.'

'Bloody robbers!'

'I've heard that a lot of properties are being revalued.'

'Anything to grub more money out of the foreigners.'

She hadn't known him in England, but didn't doubt that when he'd lived there, he'd complained about the ever-increasing rates and how they were wasted on supporting layabouts . . . It was necessary to nudge him into a better mood. 'I suppose you wouldn't like a little champagne before I get the meal.'

8

'You do, do you?'

'Well, if your stomach's so bad . . .'

'Champagne's good for the stomach.'

'Then I'll get a bottle out of the fridge and you can have a glass . . .'

'I'll have as many glasses as I like.'

'Of course you will, my pet.' It was astonishing how you could always lead a man by making him think he was doing the leading.

She returned to the kitchen and opened the double-door refrigerator, looked at the several bottles that were on one of the shelves. Champagne or cava? If she offered champagne, he'd probably complain about the cost; if cava, the fact that it wasn't champagne. In the end, she chose a bottle of Veuve Clicquot because that was her favourite. She brought the cooler out of a cupboard, slotted into this the two frozen packs which had been in the deep-freeze compartment of the refrigerator, put the bottle into the cooler and that on a tray, together with a couple of flutes.

Back in the sitting room, she set the tray on one of the occasional tables. 'Will you open it or shall I?'

'I'm feeling too rotten to do it. But don't make a mess of things and waste half of it.'

She wondered if he was genuinely ill, but regretfully decided that this appeared unlikely. 'It's terrible seeing you suffer; but you're so brave about it.'

'I'm English.'

'I met Jane at the supermarket and she asked how you were. I told her, not at all well, but that you weren't like the locals, always moaning.' Her mother had taught her that while sex brought a man running, it was polishing his ego that held him. She lifted up the bottle.

'That's champagne!'

'I thought you really needed the best.'

'Maybe. But it costs a bloody fortune.'

Full marks to her for divination! She opened the bottle without spilling a drop. 'The barman at the Ritz couldn't have done better.' She filled the two flutes, handed him

9

one, carried the second across to an armchair and sat. She stared through the French windows. Because the house and garden were on a slight downward slope, there was a view across to the Estart Caves. In a nearby field, pink almond blossom provided a swirl of colour. Jane had told her that pink trees produced bitter almonds and to eat too many of these was dangerous because they contained prussic acid. She'd fantasized about buying a couple of kilos and feeding them to Jerome, but couldn't forget that Jane was a font of misinformation . . . To look at the fields, the hills, the mountains, and the blue sky, was to recall Sunbury-by-the-river: here, all was beauty; there, all had been ugliness and even the river had been more like a sewer . . .

'What are you thinking?' he demanded.

'How lovely it is here.'

'Where it isn't ruined.'

She drained her glass. 'Would you like a refill before I go through to get lunch?'

'If you want.'

She stood, moved the occasional table with the champagne on nearer to him so that he could reach it, refilled his glass, said: 'By the way, I should be back for tea, but if I'm not I'll leave everything ready so that you have only to put the machine on the stove for coffee.'

'What are you talking about? Back from where? Where d'you think you're going?'

She said lightly: 'I told you earlier, bunnikins; before I went out to do the shopping.'

'You didn't tell me anything.'

She moved until she could bend down and nuzzle his cheek. 'I promise you I did. You were just too busy thinking great thoughts to make a note of what I told you.'

'What's it all about?'

'Theo's picking me up at half past two, which is why we're having a slightly early lunch.'

'Why are you always going out with that little toad?'

'You're always nasty about him!'

'I call a spade, a spade.'

'But he's so amusing. And he knows nearly everyone so that through him we meet more people.'

'If they're his friends, I don't want to.'

'Aren't you being just a little old-fashioned?'

'Nothing wrong with that.'

'But things have changed so. I mean, these days people can do their own thing and no one worries.'

'Which is why England's become a sink.' He drank deeply. 'Still, if you're out with him, I know what you're not doing.'

That was very amusing, but she was careful not to smile.

Theodore Lockhart enjoyed nothing more than raising someone's hackles, most especially when that someone was one of the stuffier expatriates. He had a sharp mind, a spiteful character, and a wide knowledge of modern art. He dressed with expensive taste, sported a gold Boucheron and an ornate gold medallion, drove a BMW, lived in a large flat overlooking the bay, and always claimed to be as poor as a church mouse because that caused considerable speculation as to whom was financing him.

He braked to a halt in front of Ca'n Jerome and hooted twice. The front door opened and as Karen came out and down the two steps on to the gravel, he studied her with approval. She had an attractive face and knew how to make the best of it, a slim, shapely figure which she took care to highlight without being too obvious, could talk intelligently, and was a bitch.

She opened the front passenger door and climbed in, sat.

'How is his excellency this shining day?' he asked.

She clicked her seat belt home. 'More boorish than ever because he thinks he's dying.'

'Life is seldom that generous.' He drove round in a circle, headed for the gateway. 'I'm surprised he's let you loose.'

'I told him you were taking me to see the garden with hundreds of bulbs that are out.'

'What garden's that?' He braked to a halt, checked the narrow road was clear, turned left.

'The one belonging to your Dutch friends.'

11

'Acquaintances. The Dutch are so very serious it's almost impossible to become friendly. Did he believe you?'

'Of course he did.'

'Silly man. If I were he, I wouldn't believe a single word you told me.'

'Do you have to be so beastly?'

'I was complimenting you.'

'That'll be the day.'

'Believe me . . .'

'Not a single word you tell me.'

He laughed. 'You're in good form. Why so? All excited?'

'Why not?'

'Performance seldom matches expectation . . . You do know how I hate prying into other people's affairs, don't you?'

'You spend your life doing nothing else.'

'I think you've been drinking vinegar to clear your complexion.'

She hastily pulled down the sun blind and examined her reflection in the small mirror. 'What's wrong with it?'

'Isn't that a small pimple on the tip of your nose?'

'No, it bloody well isn't.'

'Just a reflection of the sun . . . I swear I long to stay silent, but duty calls and I must answer. Do you think, my sweet, that it's a good idea to go on seeing Guido?'

'Yes.'

'Just yes?'

'Yes.'

'You don't want to know why I ask?'

'It'll be for some nasty reason.'

'I'm thinking only of your happiness. I hear things, Karen.'

'So what have you heard about Guido?'

He braked at a T-junction, turned into a lane even narrower than the one they had just left. On their right was an orange grove, on their left a field in which grew a mixture of oats and wheat that would be fed green to stock.

'Aren't you going to answer? I suppose you think I'm being stupid?'

'Never stupid. Just ill-advised.'

12

'Then whatever it is you've heard, it's crap. He's genuine with me and he's sworn he'll marry me the moment I say.'

'Sweetie, the end of the rainbow always remains just out of reach.'

'You're being sour because you're wrong.'

'I'm only thinking of you.'

'You never think of anyone but yourself.'

'You're the complete bitch!'

She turned to look at him, spoke curiously. 'Don't tell me you really are concerned on my behalf?'

He didn't answer.

'You are! You're being sweet! I think I adore you.'

He once more spoke facetiously. 'Please never say anything like that in front of my closest friends or you'll confuse them.' He had to slow down to overtake a donkey cart – a form of transport which had become very seldom met, yet only twenty years before had been ubiquitous. 'What will happen to your husband if you leave him?'

'He'll become my ex-husband.'

'I simply can't wait for the day. There's nothing more amusing than a pompous, self-satisfied, middle-aged man with horns on his head.'

CHAPTER 3

Pons silently cursed the American who had invented poker, Belmonte who'd suggested a game, and his run of bad luck. He pushed a chip into the centre, discarded three cards.

'You won't get rich on a pair,' sniggered Moya.

Like all lawyers, Moya made a fortune by exacerbating other people's miseries. Pons picked up the three cards he'd been dealt and saw to his elated surprise – since this was so against the run – that he now had a third jack. His optimism, nurtured by several glasses of wine, returned. He watched the play with great care. Only Moya and Cerda remained in and each bought just one card. So they had two pairs or were trying to fill a straight or a flush. To match one of their pairs with a singleton, or to complete the sequence, would be against the odds. For their part, they'd seen him have such useless hands throughout the evening that they'd dismiss the possibility that he had bettered this one . . .

'Throwing in?' Moya asked.

He stared at his cards with a blank expression, not an easy task since he liked to trumpet his successes because of the envy they generated.

'Make your mind up. Always assuming you've one to make.'

He pushed one of his chips forward.

'You'll have us all running for cover!'

Cerda saw him.

Moya picked up his cards, looked at them, replaced them on the table face down. 'I don't like spoiling someone's fun, but I just have to raise.' He bet four chips.

Pons wondered why lawyers always apologized before putting in the knife – to increase their pleasure? He bet his remaining six chips.

Cerda threw in.

'You've got me thinking I should be sensible and quit. But then again, maybe you're bluffing.' Moya reached round to his hip pocket, brought out his wallet and extracted a wad of ten-thousand-peseta notes. He peeled off two. 'Are you up to playing with the big boys?' A sneer curled around his words.

It abruptly became more than just a game of poker; there was now a clash of machismo.

Pons said: 'Up fifty thousand.'

Moya stared with exaggerated concentration at Pons's stake. 'I don't see that.'

'Lawyers are born three parts blind.'

'There's no bet without the money.' Moya reached out to collect the pot.

'You don't swindle me as easily as you do the foreigners. There's my property. So up fifty thousand.'

Moya fingered his weak chin that suited his scrawny, pockmarked face. 'You're putting your house and land up as security for your bet?'

'Ain't that what I said?'

He leaned back in his chair, looked around the table. 'D'you all hear him?'

No one spoke.

'We'll do this the proper way so as there's no room for complaint later on. I'll draw up the agreement and you'll all witness it.' He turned to Belmonte in whose house they were playing. 'Something to write on, Andrés, and a pen.'

Belmonte left the room, returned with a single sheet of paper and a ballpoint pen. Moya wrote rapidly, checked what he'd written, then read out: 'I, Santiago Pons Bonet, hereby testify that on the twelfth of February I pledge part or all of the property I own, known as Ca'n Ibron, as security against any debt I incur in the course of the game of cards played on the date in question. Further, I agree to settle any such debt when so requested after an interval of twenty-four hours and if unable to do so immediately will pay interest on the amount due at bank rate plus twenty per cent . . .'

'Twenty?' shouted Pons, outraged.

'Credit is always expensive.' He pushed the paper across. 'Sign and we will all witness.'

Despite the burning need to win to make a fool of Moya and the effects of the wine he had drunk, Pons hesitated. The building trade was suffering a downturn, his company was cash-light, the mortgage repayments on the house were making life difficult, and he was in no position to suffer even a moderate financial loss . . .

'I always said your tongue's bigger than your cojones,' Moya sneered.

The slur on his manhood swept away all Pons's caution. He grabbed the pen and signed.

When the paper was returned to Moya, he examined it carefully before placing it under his pile of counters. He counted out ten notes. 'There's your fifty thousand and another fifty.'

'And another hundred thousand.'

'Your hundred and another hundred.' He counted his remaining money and found it to be insufficient for the bet.

Pons gleefully thumped a fist down on the table. 'I can't see two hundred thousand, I can't, not even with my eyes wide open. Seems like your tongue is a sight bigger than your pocket!'

'I can cover the bet a thousand times over.'

'Not without security, you can't.'

'Security? I've enough of that to buy the lot of you out and just wonder what's happened to my small change.'

'Because you're a swindler. But you're not swindling me. Security, or the game's mine.'

Moya swore at some length, but with little variety. Then he told Belmonte to bring him another piece of paper. When he had this, he wrote rapidly. 'There you are!'

Pons reached out and picked it up. 'Let's see the one I just signed.'

'Why?'

'To make certain this is the same and you ain't trying anything.'

Moya threw the first agreement across the table.

Pons took a long time comparing the two. Finally, he said: 'The signatures ain't the same.'

Moya suggested he did something generally considered to be impossible.

Pons passed the paper around for it to be witnessed. When it was returned to him, he said: 'Your hundred thousand and another hundred thousand.'

'And another.'

'And another.'

'And half a million.'

'And a million.'

The onlookers were gripped by the same feverish tension – occasionally referred to as the curse of the Mallorquins – as the two players; Belmonte began to breathe rapidly through his mouth, as if he'd been running, Cerdo was sweating . . .

Moya's legal work had taught him that, no matter how emotionally involved he became, he must always retain sufficient self-control to be able to see where his own interests lay. He could afford to increase the stake almost indefinitely. But Pons had been having bad cards all night and so his present confidence argued that he finally had a good hand, perhaps even a full house or four of a kind. In which case, he would never fold, however high the stake was raised. And he – Moya – might lose a fortune to an oaf who never lost the chance to insult him. 'See you.'

There was a collective sigh – an expression of relief that the tension would not increase, of regret that it would not.

Pons exposed his three jacks with a hand that trembled.

'You're that good!' Moya sounded overwhelmed.

'That's right. Gets a bit painful playing with the big boys, don't it?' Pons reached out to take the pot.

'Hang on.'

'What for?'

'Doesn't a straight beat three of a kind?'

'You ain't got a straight!'

Moya exposed his hand. 'Just not your lucky night! How

much does it all add up to? Was it something over two million?'

Completed just over two years previously, Ca'n Ibron lacked no luxury other than planning permission. Set in the middle of a couple of hectares of good land, it provided the perfect home for a family.

Pons drove into the garage too quickly and had to brake very hard to avoid ramming the end wall. He climbed out of the car before he realized he'd left the lights on, leaned back in and lost his balance to collapse across the driving seat. Concentrating very hard, he switched off the lights, stood, weaved his way between the car and the wall to the outside where he came to an unsteady stop. Much wine had been drunk after Moya had left Belmonte's home; had words been daggers, Moya would have arrived home a bloody corpse.

The moon was almost full and the sky was cloudless. He stared at the rock-faced house and remembered the party they'd given days after they'd moved in. A whole salmon, two suckling pigs, ham, chorizo and sobrassada delicacies, three different types of Spanish omelettes, brawn . . . Friends had said they'd never seen such a spread. He turned to look at Cristina's garden, in the moonlight a place of mysterious forms, and thought of the pleasure she gained from tending it and the fun Rosa and Lucía had in the summer in the splash pool beyond the shade tree. An inner voice began to shout. No one was going to take all this away from him, least of all a runt of a thieving lawyer . . .

He crossed to the covered patio. He opened the heavy, panelled wooden door, went inside and almost forgot to close and lock it. He climbed the stairs to their bedroom, which he tried to enter silently, an attempt which failed when he became entangled with a chair and crashed to the floor. The overhead light went on.

He struggled to his feet. 'The chair moved and made me fall,' he said, his speech heavy.

'It simply won't stay still.' Cristina sat upright.

His parents, bewildered by her vivacious sense of humour

and light-hearted approach to life, spoke about her as their son's foreign wife. It was true that her mother was French, but her father was Mallorquin and she had been born and lived all her life on the island.

He picked up the chair, almost overbalancing in doing so. 'Did you drive back?'

'You think I walked?'

'It looks very unlikely . . . I do wish you wouldn't drive when you've drunk so much.'

Many would have shouted at her to keep her trap shut and what her husband drank was his affair. But she was emotional and became very upset if he spoke roughly to her.

'Do you want something to eat?'

'No.' He began to undress.

She settled back and turned on her side.

After some confusion, he managed to put on his pyjamas and climb into bed. As he switched off the light, a hand briefly rested on his chest. 'Sweet dreams, my love,' she said.

He stared into the darkness and suffered black thoughts. How could he have been such a fool? Had he not promised himself at the beginning of the game that if he lost all his chips, he'd quit? How could he have put Cristina's, Rosa's, and Lucía's future happiness at risk? What kind of a bastard husband was he?

He tried to ease his misery. The bank would lend him the money to pay his gambling losses. Yet no sooner had he assured himself of that than he accepted it was virtually certain they would not. Building was in the doldrums and that made things very difficult for his company which, as did so many these days, ran on borrowed money and the current overdraft was too high – as the bank kept reminding him. The house would have provided very good security, but for Carlos . . . He cursed his brother who had always been weak and had become mixed up with a bunch of no-gooders. A year before, he'd defrauded a family friend of many millions of pesetas. The victim had generously said he wouldn't call in the police provided he was repaid the money. Carlos couldn't repay it as he had already squandered it. His parents couldn't repay it because they had little capital. They had come to their 'rich' son and begged him to find the money because they could not contemplate the thought of Carlos's being sent to jail. He'd mortgaged the house to raise the money. He'd not told Cristina because he was certain she wouldn't, couldn't, understand how he could risk his own family's happiness for a brother he held in contempt, too emotionally upset to realize it was his parents he was protecting . . . He'd just have to find work. A rich foreigner who wanted a house built quickly . . . Zavala! That mega-rich, snake-smooth Bolivian who'd wanted an extension to his already palatial mansion and to whom he'd given an estimate. It had been an honest estimate – for a foreigner – but Zavala, with the miserly instincts of the really wealthy, had gone on and on trying to beat down the price until he'd finally said to find someone else who'd do the job at a loss. But if he now went back and meekly agreed a revised estimate, perhaps he could still secure the job. He'd save on labour by working on site from dawn to dusk. That would be a start. And Zavala, who must mix with the other rich on the island, would say he was employing a builder who worked like a demon and did a first-class job at a very reasonable price. They, in turn, would call on him to do work for them since the rich never suffered downturns . . .

Optimism, aided by the wine, prevailed. His firm would prosper until he had paid off Moya and the overdraft, cleared the mortgage. He'd buy Cristina a little red Ford Ka and throw a party for Rosa's First Communion that would arouse the envy of all their friends . . .

He fell asleep and began to snore.

CHAPTER 4

July was so hot that many tourists on the beaches sought shade. Alvarez sat at his desk, sweated, and stared at the unopened mail, some of which dated back several days. Dolores was in one of her bad moods and neither Jaime nor he could work out what had so upset her – a question of importance since the impact on their lives was considerable. Only that morning, he had come down to breakfast to be offered only half a yesterday's barra to accompany the hot chocolate. When he'd asked her, very pleasantly, why she hadn't earlier bought him an ensaimada, she'd hissed that she wasn't working herself into the grave for someone so lazy that the only thing he was good at was telling other people what to do . . .

The phone rang.

It was a time of the morning when people frequently tried to pass on their troubles . . .

The phone ceased ringing. As the old adage said, Forget trouble and trouble will forget you.

Except that some troubles were too serious to be forgotten. Neither he nor Jaime had said anything to Dolores that could have offended – they had long since learned to keep their opinions of women's strange foibles to themselves. Isabel and Juan had recently been unusually well-behaved . . .

The phone resumed ringing. Trouble may forget you, but never for long enough. It could, of course, be the superior chief – a typically suspicious Madrileño – checking he was hard at work . . . He answered the call.

'Are you the inspector?' a woman asked, her speech hurried. 'The doctor says you're to come right away.'

When a man became a doctor, he often thought himself ennobled. 'What gives him that idea?'

'What idea?'

'That he can order me around.'

There was a long pause. 'The señor's dead.'

The speaker's distressed confusion was clear and his tone became more friendly. 'Tell me his name.'

'Señor Zavala.'

'And the doctor who's examined him believes there is cause for doubting he died a natural death?'

Another silence. 'All I know is, he told me to ring the Cuerpo.'

'Are you speaking from the señor's house?'

'That's right.'

'Where is it and what's its name?'

'Son Fuyell. It's in Cardona Valley.'

'That lies outside my area,' he said with satisfaction. 'If you ring Inspector Catany . . .'

'But I did. He said to get in touch with you because you'd deal with things.'

Catany was one of those men who was forever trying to avoid doing his duty. 'The best thing to do is to get back on to him and explain that Cardona Valley lies within his area.'

'He said this was your responsibility because the house is on the east side of the valley.'

He'd forgotten that the line dividing the fiefs ran along the centre of the valley. 'What's the doctor's name?' he asked, his tone expressing his annoyance.

'I . . . I've forgotten. I mean, it's all been such a shock. There was me and Susana doing the work as usual and Lorenzo comes in and says the señor's dead. I thought it was just one of his nasty jokes and –'

He interrupted the breathless flow of words. 'Tell the doctor I'll be along as soon as possible.'

He replaced the receiver, looked at his watch. Merienda time. He made his way downstairs, where he spoke to the duty cabo. 'If anyone wants me, tell 'em I've been called out.'

'To the nearest bar?'

Cabos were not only becoming younger, they were growing ever more insolent.

In the Club Llueso, the barman, without being asked, poured out a brandy and passed the glass across, then clamped a measure of coffee on to the espresso machine.

Alvarez crossed to a window table and sat. He lit a cigarette and stared at the tourists who were making their way up or down the steps which joined the two levels of the square. Two attractive young women, wearing bikini tops and very short shorts, came down the steps. He could remember the time when it had been exciting to gain a flashing glimpse of the flesh above the knee. Little more than twenty years before, girlie magazines brought into the country by tourists had been forfeited by the airport guardia (who had enjoyed the photographs), yet now one could go into many newsagents and openly buy magazines and videos that amazed one's imagination . . .

The barman put a cup of coffee on the table. 'You look like you've lost something.'

'My youth.'

'If you ever find it, let us know how to do the same.'

Alvarez poured the remaining brandy into the coffee. 'You can fill this up again.' He held out the glass.

'That won't help you get any younger.'

'But it'll make getting older seem less painful.'

The range of mountains which stretched from west to east was often referred to as the backbone of the island; accepting that description, then Cardona Valley, whose mouth was almost a kilometre from the village of Cardona, lay between two of the ribs (which numbered very many more than twelve). The valley ended at the base of a nine-hundred-metre mountain and so offered access to nowhere; the soil was poor and mostly rocky and there were few farms. It was a place of solitude and there could be few greater contrasts than between there and the concrete jungles which engulfed much of the coast.

Alvarez drove into the valley, past rocks which had been striated by the weather and had the surfaces of a washboard.

He slowed, enjoying the nearly empty land and the stark mountain faces. Here was a land and a way of life that had been lost elsewhere.

The narrow, dusty road hugged the eastern side of the valley and the few farms he passed were to his left. His sense of peace became disturbed as he wondered if Inspector Catany had pulled a fast one on him? If so . . .

An elaborate gateway with wrought-iron gates – barbarically anomalous in such surroundings – appeared to his right and on each gatepost was the name Son Fuyell. At this point in the valley, the east side was lower and far less precipitous than the west side and the dirt track from the gateway passed a small copse of trees before it climbed fairly easily up to a plateau, in the centre of which was a very large house. He parked behind another car and climbed out on to the drive. If he were called on to design heaven, this would be how it would look. To the west, mountains, their jagged crests cutting into the sky; to the north, more mountains, each slightly higher than the one in front, so that they resembled a child's drawing; to the east, hills that flowed away; to the south, a view of the central plain and, if one had imagination, the distant sea. And if such natural beauty were not enough, there was a breeze, so slight it hardly ruffled the hairs on his head, yet sufficient to lessen the worst of the heat.

He crossed to the front door, set under an elegant porch, and rang the bell. The door was opened by a young woman whose red eyes and strained expression testified to a disturbed emotional state. She said nothing, just stared at him. He introduced himself, stepped inside. The large hall, cool thanks to air-conditioning, was remarkable for four large, framed paintings which to him were such a meaningless jumble of shapes and colours that he felt certain they were by some highly regarded artist. 'I'm afraid you've had a nasty shock,' he said comfortingly.

It had been a terrible shock. There'd been no sight of the señor, but neither she nor Susana had thought anything of that; then Lorenzo had arrived at the house to say the señor was at the bottom of the pool . . . She began to cry.

Alvarez consoled her as best he could, and when she'd regained some self-control, he asked her where the doctor was. She did not know. 'Perhaps he's by the pool. What's my best way of getting there?'

To the south of the house, the land sloped gently for a couple of hundred metres before it dived away, and the swimming pool, backed by a considerable complex on one side, was several metres lower. As he crossed the lawn, he could look down and see that a man, dressed in a light-coloured linen suit, was seated in the shade of the main area of the complex. When the other turned, he recognized him. Definitely not his lucky day!

'You've finally managed to get here?' was Dr Sanz's greeting.

'I'm afraid I was delayed . . .'

'I have been waiting more than an hour and a quarter.'

'It was very important . . .'

'My time is far too valuable to waste.'

Doctors, especially those like Sanz, considered their time to be more valuable than rubies. 'Señor Zavala drowned in the pool?'

'Isn't that obvious?'

'I haven't yet had time to look . . .'

'Time clearly has no priority for you.'

'Why do you think this may not have been an accident?'

'I have expressed no such thought.'

'But since you've called me here . . .'

'Because of the facts.'

'What facts are those?'

'Have you not spoken to the staff?'

'Not yet. It seemed best to speak to you first so that you wouldn't be held here any longer than absolutely necessary.'

Sanz looked at him with sharp dislike. 'Yesterday evening, the younger maid saw a car drive down to the road at a speed that was obviously reckless. Since there may be considerable significance in that fact, I deemed it advisable for the Cuerpo to be present when the body is recovered and examined.'

Alvarez rubbed his chin and discovered that he had forgotten to shave that morning. 'Where was she when she saw the car?'

'It is not my job to question her.'

'What sort of time was this?'

'I can only repeat what I have just said in the hope that you will eventually understand.'

Alvarez took a pace forward towards the edge of the pool, came to a stop when Sanz said: 'Do you see the chair, there?' He pointed at the painted metal patio chair that lay on its side. 'There's a stain on it which is almost certainly dried blood.'

Alvarez crossed to the chair. Near the centre of the top of the back was a dull, rust-coloured, shapeless stain that continued round and out of sight where the chair was in contact with the tiled ground. Blood changed colour quickly in hot sun. 'I'll check if it is blood,' he said, hoping that the doctor would resent this implied doubt.

He walked on to the edge of the pool. At the bottom of the deep end lay a man, dressed in sleeveless shirt and flannel trousers, face downwards, one arm outstretched, the other tucked under himself. His long brown hair was spread out and gave the disturbing impression of a halo. Alvarez mentally shivered. To look at death was to see one's future . . . He spoke to Sanz who had left the shade and joined him. 'I'll call the guardia to come and retrieve the body, then you can make a preliminary examination.'

'I can't waste any more time here. Strip off and get it out.'

'I would, but orders say that bodies not readily accessible have to be recovered by the special unit.' There was no such bureaucratic regulation, but Alvarez was betting that Sanz would not know that.

CHAPTER 5

Photographs had been taken, the area had been searched – nothing of any significance had been found – and Sanz had completed his examination of the body.

'There is every reason to believe he died from drowning, despite the wound to his head,' Sanz said, having returned from washing his hands in the small bathroom to the right of the pool complex. 'There's the fine froth in the nostrils and mouth which I pointed out – a common mark of drowning.'

Death was unnerving, its marks even more so. Alvarez stared longingly at the many bottles on the shelf behind the bar.

'Petechiae are absent, which again points to drowning. But to be certain as to the cause of death, naturally you will await the results of the PM.'

'Can you give a time of death?'

'Between seven and nine last night. A figure which I hope you can appreciate is little more than an educated estimate when the body has been immersed in water at a temperature of around thirty degrees.'

'And you don't think the head wound was serious?'

'Kindly do not keep putting words into my mouth. I said that although the skin was torn and there had been generous bleeding, I did not believe the skull had been fractured or that he had been rendered unconscious. However, the effect or effects of injury sustained to the skull are virtually impossible to evaluate in the absence of a PM.' Sanz paused. 'Indeed, it is not long since I treated a man who'd fallen from a bicycle and seemed to be suffering from no more than a twisted ankle and slight bruising of the skull. There was no reason to suspect his injury was any more serious than that. No reason whatsoever.'

Alvarez thought that this emphasis might well indicate a mistaken diagnosis. Even Homer nodded.

There was a long pause before Sanz, a note of annoyance in his voice, confirmed Alvarez's suspicions. 'Later, while working, he collapsed and died. The autopsy showed a large clot of blood had accumulated beneath the skull at the site of the bruise. Naturally, you will appreciate that there was absolutely no way of predetermining the possibility.'

Alvarez uneasily remembered a stumble on the stairs he had suffered a week previously. Although his head had hit the wall, it had not done so with sufficient force even to raise a small bump. But clearly there were dangers to the slightest blow. How long did the threat of a blood clot continue?

'Have you made arrangements for the body to be transported to the Institute?' Sanz asked curtly, annoyed by Alvarez's gaucherie in not expressing a certainty that there could not possibly have been the slightest lack of professional skill.

'They should be here any minute.'

'Then finally I can leave.'

'If you wouldn't mind telling me something?'

'Which is?'

'Your judgement of what might have happened.'

'I never speculate.' Sanz picked up his medical bag and left.

Alvarez stared at the fallen chair. If Zavala had fallen on to it, as seemed likely, what had caused him to trip? The doctor doubted he'd been knocked unconscious, but he might have been dazed and staggered across the patio to tumble into the pool. But on a level with the chair, the water was no deeper than one metre twenty. However dazed, surely an instinctive self-preservation would have made certain he stood up?

Two men bundled the dead man into a body bag. The younger looked up the gently sloping land. 'We ought to have brought the van down here.'

'Take life more quietly at night and you'd have some energy for the morning,' said the elder man. 'Come on, get moving.'

They picked up the bag and left. Alvarez envied them their lack of reverential fear for death.

He made his way up to the front door and arrived in time to see the van drive off. The front door was unlocked and he opened it, stepped into the hall, and called out. Susana, a middle-aged woman, came through the doorway to the right. Initially, her manner was constrained – she had a typical islander's distrust of authority – but Alvarez's easy, friendly manner, and the fact that his accent marked him as a local, quickly gained her confidence.

'You'd best come into the kitchen so as I can make some coffee.'

He followed her through a doorway, along a short passage, and into a kitchen, notable for its size and wealth of domestic machines. He sat in the small eating area and, as she prepared the coffee machine, listened with the endless patience of a peasant as she repeatedly told him how shocked she and Inés had been when Lorenzo had rushed into the house and told them the señor was at the bottom of the swimming pool. At first, they'd thought he was joking. He had a cruel sense of humour. There was the time he'd told Inés he'd taken a photo of her and sent it to a magazine. Why was that cruel? The señor had been away, the day had been hotter than ever and Inés had decided to go for a swim. Being of the younger generation, lacking both a sense of shame and a costume, she'd stripped off and swum naked. Lorenzo, who never missed a thing, had seen her when he'd returned from the other end of the property where he was mending a fence. He was certain the magazine would pay heavily for such delightful snaps. Inés had called him many names before he finally admitted he was joking and said he hadn't realized she wasn't just swimming topless like so many did. But one had only to have seen the gleam in his eyes to know that he'd seen more than he was now admitting . . .

Susana opened a tin and put some biscuits on a plate,

carried the plate over to where Alvarez sat. 'I made these yesterday for the señor, but he won't be eating them now, God rest his soul.'

The coffee machine hissed and she lifted it off the stove, poured the contents into two mugs. After putting milk and sugar on the table, she sat opposite him.

He asked her why it was that neither she nor Inés had been surprised not to have seen Zavala in the morning, since it was quite late before his body had been discovered.

'It's like this. I live in the staff house that's out of sight on the other side of the hill – I reckon it was built there so as no one could tell what was going on here. Inés is with her parents in the village and Lorenzo has his own finca. So I'm around early in the morning, but the señor used to get up at all times and he might want breakfast, he might not. We never knew when to expect to see him. Didn't think anything when there was no sign of him. And to think he was at the bottom of the pool!' She sucked in her breath in a gesture of shocked surprise.

'What kind of a man was he to work for?'

'Same as most,' she answered carefully.

He smiled. 'Difficult?'

'I've never met one that wasn't some of the time. But I suppose he wasn't too bad for a foreigner, if one takes everything into account.'

'He wasn't Spanish?'

'You didn't know?'

'I've not had the chance to find out things yet. Where was he from?'

'South America. Couldn't miss it when he spoke.' Her tone was critical. Like distant relations, South Americans were condemned for faults that could seldom be specified.

'Which country?'

'Bolivia.'

'How long has he lived here?'

'A year, maybe a little more. He bought the place from the family of a German who had it built and then died suddenly. Not a lucky house.'

30

'Certainly doesn't seem to be. Must have cost a few pesetas?'

'They do say the señor paid four hundred million. But that's impossible. Who has that much money to pay for a house?'

'If he was that wealthy, I reckon he thought his money really made him someone?'

He had gained her confidence and his last remark persuaded her to describe Zavala in less flattering and more realistic terms. He had been arrogant, bad-tempered, very quick to complain, very slow to praise. There had been times when she'd been tempted to throw in the job, but she was a widow and she had no man to keep her. Her beloved husband had died several years previously . . .

He listened sympathetically as he ate a second biscuit; then, when she became silent, he picked up a third one. 'These are really delicious!'

'The señor liked them, which is why I was always making them. Inés said that maybe one day she'd put some rat poison in the mixture . . . Sweet Mary!' She put her hand to her mouth.

'Don't worry, he didn't die from poison.'

'She was joking. You must understand that.'

'Of course I do.'

'I told her to leave that kind of joke to Lorenzo, but . . . Well, she was upset.'

'For any particular reason?'

She hesitated. 'You won't tell her I've said?'

'My lips will be sealed.'

'When she started working here, I said to watch out because she's good-looking and the señor was after the women even more than most men are. Maybe he'd leave her alone because she was a servant, but maybe he'd think that gave him the right to take what he wanted. She was in the television room, dusting, and he went in and started telling her how good-looking she was. She's no fool – even if she did swim naked – and knew what he was after, but couldn't think what to do. It's not easy when a man pays the wages. So he seemed to think she was listening and got busy with his hands. Then the phone rang and when he went to answer it, she cleared out. It's after that when she joked about the rat poison. You do understand, don't you?'

'Of course.'

Susana finished the coffee in her mug. 'He didn't try again and acted like it had never happened. Inés couldn't understand that. I said it was maybe that that phone call had been one of his women saying she was waiting and since he was going to get what he was after, Inés just became a servant again.'

'More than likely. I take it there's no Señora Zavala?'

'If there is one, she's never been near here. And who'd blame her for staying away when he acted like he did?'

'Has he had a particular girlfriend very recently?'

She picked up a biscuit and nibbled it. 'There's been one up here several times – a real bitch!'

'Why d'you say that?'

'She's married. It's one thing to have fun when you're on your own – not that we did in my time – it's another to spit in your husband's bed.'

'How do you know she's married?'

'She didn't wear a wedding ring.'

'I don't follow that. If she didn't wear one . . .'

'What I mean is, she arrived here with nothing on her finger, but I've eyes and can see the two bands of light flesh where she's normally got the engagement and wedding rings.'

'What's her name?'

'Karen.'

'And her surname?'

She shrugged her shoulders.

'Have you any idea of her nationality?'

'English. Not that I needed her to tell me that – not with the disgusting way she behaves.'

'D'you know where she lives?'

'How would I?'

He helped himself to another biscuit and, knowing that the

surest way to a middle-aged woman's heart was not to tell her she was beautiful, but to praise her cooking, said again how delicious it was.

For a brief moment she was pleased, but then was once more worried. 'It is an accident what happened, isn't it?'

'There's nothing to say it wasn't.'

'It's just that with you asking all these questions, I've been wondering.'

'There are always problems which have to be sorted out when someone dies unexpectedly. And I'm afraid there are a few more things I have to know. Tell me about yesterday evening.'

'How d'you mean?'

'When did you last see the señor, did he say if he was expecting anyone to visit, do you know if anyone did come here; anything that'll help me picture how things were.'

'But I told you, I don't know what went on because I can't see the big house from my place.'

'And you were in your house all evening?'

'I don't work when I don't have to.'

He smiled. 'Who does? What exactly were your working hours?'

She explained, at considerable length because she kept diverting, sometimes to the point where it was difficult to remember the thread of the conversation. Times had not exactly been fixed and if she had to work more than usual, she made certain she had time off to compensate, however much the señor complained. She walked up to the big house to arrive at seven-thirty. If he wanted breakfast, either she or Inés – who was meant to arrive at eight, but seldom did, being of a generation who had no idea what work really meant – prepared that. She spent most of the morning in the kitchen, but if necessary and there was the time, gave Inés a hand with the housework.

The señor had been very fond of fish and shellfish, so she had specialized in cooking fish dishes. He seldom praised, but more than once he'd told her that her Rape en salsa de mariscos was the best he'd ever eaten. In the afternoon, she naturally had a siesta. She made coffee – although occasionally he wanted tea – and served this with biscuits at six in the evenings. He said whether he wanted supper; often, he did not because he was going out. If he was entertaining guests, then she had to cook a hot meal . . .

'What happened about the evening meal yesterday?'

'He couldn't make up his mind, that's what happened.'

'Tell me about it.'

'When I served the coffee, he said he was going out and didn't want anything. Then, when I collected the dirty things, he'd changed his mind and was staying in and wanted something cold. Later on, he phoned and said he wasn't certain what he'd be doing and would let me know when he did.'

'There's an internal phone system and you have a receiver in your house?'

'How else d'you think?'

'I have to make doubly certain because I have a superior chief who asks more unnecessary questions than a dog has fleas. Would you know what the time was when he phoned you?'

'Half past seven. He said he'd ring back at eight and tell me for certain. Didn't matter what happened to my evening, of course . . .' She stopped abruptly.

He guessed she was castigating herself for her criticism. 'You know, the way a person acts isn't altered by his dying. You're helping me by saying how things really were.'

'It's just . . . I mean, if he could have decided earlier, I'd have known how my evening was going to be. Only . . . he wasn't the kind of man to think of other people.' She had spoken hurriedly as if trying to race her conscience.

'Did he ring you later on?'

'No. Couldn't be bothered.'

'Then you spent the evening uncertain whether or not you'd have to return to work?'

'I ain't daft. I waited, then rang back to find out if he'd made his mind up.'

'And had he?'

'I wouldn't know. There was no answer. Rang three times,

34

then I thought to hell with it, he could get his own supper.'

'What was the time when you phoned him?'

'Eight. When he'd said he'd phone me.'

'Presumably there's a phone down at the pool house?'

''Course there is. Phones everywhere. I'd have given something to be able to get rid of the one in my place so as he couldn't have bothered me all the time.'

'Did it puzzle you that he didn't answer your call?'

'No. Just thought he'd decided to go out and couldn't be bothered to tell me.' She hesitated, then added: 'If I'd gone to find out why he didn't answer . . .' She became silent, her expression strained.

'You'd no reason to think you ought to check, had you?'

'Of course I hadn't. There've been times enough when he didn't do what he said he would.'

'Then you've absolutely no reason to blame yourself.'

'It's just I can't help thinking.'

'Sometimes, it pays not to think.'

'Easy to say.' She sighed.

The time of death could seldom, if ever, be medically estimated with any firm degree of accuracy, but when a figure was given, it could be accepted unless or until there was reason to doubt it. Dr Sanz had placed the time of death at between seven and nine. Zavala had spoken to Susana at half past seven, had failed to answer the phone at eight even though she had rung three times. There was here reason to believe death had occurred between half-seven and eight . . .

'There's one last thing. I need to talk to Inés.'

'She's not here. She was so upset I told her to go off back home. I mean, I didn't think you might want to speak to her. If I'd known . . .'

'Don't worry. Tell me where she lives and I'll see her there.'

'You . . . you won't mention what I told you about her in the television room, will you? She's scared her novio will hear about it. He's the jealous type and would likely start wondering if she'd been smiling at the señor.'

'Could she have been?'

For several seconds, Susana hesitated, then she said: 'When youngsters see foreigners who are rich beyond understanding, likely they have silly ideas.'

'And who can blame 'em . . . So if you'll give me her address?'

'The house is in Carrer Magallanes, but I can't say the number.'

'I'll soon find out what that is.' He looked up at the electric clock on the far wall. 'I'd better start moving.'

'There's still some biscuits left.'

He reached across the table.

CHAPTER 6

Jaime was seated at the table in the dining/sitting room, a bottle of brandy and a glass in front of him. Alvarez looked at the bead curtain across the kitchen doorway, from behind which came the sounds of cooking. He said in a low voice: 'How are things now?'

'A little while back, she was singing,' Jaime replied.

Alvarez sat, reached down and opened the sideboard to bring out a tumbler. He poured himself a generous brandy. 'Didn't you get some ice?'

'No.'

It was obvious that Jaime had foregone ice in order to avoid a face-to-face confrontation with his wife. Man or mouse? Alvarez wondered sarcastically.

Dolores began to sing once more.

Singing could indicate many moods and it might be dangerously mistaken to assume that she was expressing contentment. He listened to the words, but although her voice was true, her enunciation was not and it took him time to understand that a young lady in Seville had looked down into the street from her protected eyrie and meeting the gaze of a handsome young man had felt the strings of her heart plucked . . . Was the handsome young man honourable or heartless? Nothing annoyed Dolores more than men who took advantage of emotionally helpless women . . . She did not finish the song.

He looked at his glass, then at the bead curtain. A warm brandy was preferable to no brandy, but less welcome than a cold one. Yet to go through to the kitchen for ice might well provoke her annoyance, especially if the song would have ended with betrayal . . .

The strings of beads parted as she looked into the room. 'So you're both back!'

Nervously, they nodded.

'Where are the children?'

'I haven't seen them,' Jaime muttered.

'They won't be far away. Lunch will be in a few minutes.' She withdrew.

Her tone had been warm and she had not condemned their drinking. Alvarez stood. 'If you won't get some ice, I will.' He went through to the kitchen. 'I thought Madonna must be in here,' he said, as he opened a cupboard and brought out the small ice container.

'What are you talking about?' she asked.

'When I heard the singing, I reckoned it had to be her.'

'Must you say such stupid things?' she asked, clearly flattered.

He opened the refrigerator and brought out a plastic tray of ice, pressed out the cubes. 'What's for lunch?'

'Conill amb ceba.'

'A feast!'

'Perhaps.'

'When you do the cooking, nothing less.' He replaced the tray in the refrigerator, picked up the ice bucket, returned to the dining room. As he sat, he said: 'Lunch is conill amb ceba.' He dropped four cubes of ice into his glass.

Jaime drained his glass. 'This morning her tongue was like a knife, now she cooks one of my favourite dishes.' He poured himself another drink. 'I tell you, I'll be dead and buried and still not begin to understand her. How do you ever know where you are with a woman?'

'You don't, which is why they've got us by the short and curlies.'

'If we changed our minds as often as they do, we'd be dizzy.'

The front door banged and there was a clatter of feet on the tiled floors. Juan ran into the room, followed by Isabel. 'What's grub?' he asked loudly, as he came to a stop.

Dolores stepped through the bead curtains. 'Lunch is almost ready, so you two can lay the table.'

'That's a girl's job,' Juan said.

'Boys always help.'

'Dad and Uncle never do.'

Jaime stared angrily at his son.

'When men work hard, they need to have time to rest.' She withdrew.

Jaime leaned forward until the table pressed into his stomach. 'It's weird!'

Alvarez nodded. However, the circumstances being what they were, they should heed the old Mallorquin saying, When the almond crop is heavy, eat all you can because next year there may be none. He drained his glass, refilled it.

Carrer Magallanes was a narrow road on the outskirts of Cardona, and number seventeen was on the eastern side, one of a line of terrace houses that directly fronted the road. From the outside it looked nondescript and, with all shutters closed against the heat, deserted; inside, was a home enjoying many of the luxuries that the success of the tourist trade had brought to the island.

Inés, far more composed than she had been that morning, was dressed in a brightly coloured frock that was sufficiently close fitting to show she was not yet troubled by the excess weight which so often affected the women of the island. 'I'm in a hurry,' she said with nervous impatience.

'It won't take a moment for you to answer a couple of questions,' Alvarez answered.

'Why? I mean, I didn't even know the señor had had an accident until Lorenzo told us.'

'D'you mind if I sit down? I've had a heavy day and my legs are tired.'

As was so often the case, the front room was for formal occasions and the furniture had been chosen for appearance, not comfort. The wooden chair with a rush seat and an elaborately shaped back dug into him however much he moved around. 'When I was talking to Dr Sanz, he mentioned the

39

fact that you'd told him you'd seen a car drive away from Son Fuyell last night. Obviously this might be important, so I need to know more about it. What was the time?'

She fidgeted with her fingers.

'Was it before or after dark?'

She spoke so hurriedly that the words jostled each other. 'I was all shocked. I mean, first me and Susana thought Lorenzo was joking, then we found he wasn't. And when the doctor came, he started asking questions and it was like he was blaming us . . . I just didn't know what I was saying.'

'Are you now suggesting you didn't see a car leaving Son Fuyell last night?'

She looked longingly at the front door.

'Perhaps you were with a friend?'

She opened her mouth to speak, closed it.

'If you were, where's the harm?'

'Mum and Dad don't like him,' she said sullenly.

'That's far from unusual. Lots of parents dislike their daughters' friends for no good reason.'

'They won't listen.'

'Once again, quite normal.'

'They're so old-fashioned. Expect me to be back home in the evening when everyone else is out having fun.'

'They worry you might be having the kind of fun that maybe they had when they were young.' In presenting himself as a modern liberal, he ignored the certainty that when her parents had been young, the rules of behaviour might have been lax for a son, but certainly had not been so for a daughter. 'At a guess, you and your boyfriend found somewhere nice and quiet to be on your own?'

She nodded.

'Near Son Fuyell?'

She nodded again.

'Where exactly?'

'There are some trees just inside the entrance . . .' She stopped.

'I remember them; a small copse of pines.'

'Well . . . There's a bit of a clearing just inside them which

40

is big enough for a car. Me and Francisco often . . . sometimes go there to . . . to listen to the nightingales.'

He managed not to smile.

'Nothing ever happens.'

'When you parked amongst the pines, was it dark?'

'Not really, because of the moon.'

'But it would have been but for the moon?'

The question puzzled her until he rephrased it. She agreed it had been after dark.

'How long were you there before you saw this other car?'

'A bit of time.'

'You couldn't be more definite?'

She shook her head.

'What made you notice it?'

'I thought maybe it was the señor and was kind of worried he might notice us. Only he couldn't have. And anyway, his car's a cabriolet and he always has the top down. Another thing, it was going so fast. Francisco said it was like the driver didn't care what happened to the car. I mean, that track isn't exactly smooth.'

'Can you say what kind it was?'

'I don't know one from another, not like Francisco. If he wins the lottery, he's going to buy a BMW and take me everywhere in it.'

'It seems you were able to see the car pretty clearly, but how's that when you'd driven into the clearing and must have been facing the wrong way?'

There was a long silence during which her face reddened.

'Perhaps,' he suggested, 'it was a little cramped in the car, so you moved out of it?'

'We just sat. Nothing happened.'

He thought it more likely that the nightingales had been singing loudly.

CHAPTER 7

Inés, very reluctantly, had given Alvarez her novio's address, but when he spoke to Francisco's mother, she said that her son had driven off without telling her where he was going and she'd no idea where he might be. Alvarez assured her that although this was a police matter, her son was in no way directly involved and he finally persuaded her to surmise that Francisco might have driven down to Port Llueso to meet his pals and waste his time and money in a bar. Did Francisco favour any particular bar? Her son was like her husband and favoured them all.

Alvarez returned to his car and sat behind the wheel. There were almost as many bars in the port as politicians in hell and tracing Francisco Ferriol could prove to be a very long task. But time was moving on and soon Dolores would start preparing supper. When in a sunny mood, nothing gave her greater pleasure than to give full rein to her genius and it might even be that she would be cooking Bacalao al cava rosado – a mixture of fish, wine, cream, onion, mushrooms, nuts, and black pepper, that in her hands became a culinary masterpiece. But it had to be remembered that it was a dish which needed to be eaten as soon as it was cooked; a portion kept warm for a latecomer would become a shadow of its true self. Clearly, logic demanded that Ferriol be questioned another day. Unfortunately, matters other than logic had to be considered. Since there was to be a PM on Zavala, the superior chief would be advised of that fact, probably already had been. Salas expected everything to be done as soon as the need to do it arose; he invariably treated excuses, even genuine ones, with gross insensitiveness . . . Regretfully, Alvarez decided he was going to have to risk a spoiled meal.

Material greed had led men to do their best to destroy the charm of Bahia de Llueso, but their best had not yet been good enough. The bay backed by mountains and marshland, the cerulean sea, and the curving beaches of sand, pebbles, or rock, were still beautiful despite the marina, flats, restaurants, and stores selling kitschy goods and the holiday camp which looked as if it had been designed by a French bureaucrat. However depressed, he had only to drive down to the port and stare out at the natural beauty to feel refreshed.

Since a group of young Mallorquin men would be looking for nubile tourists, he first checked the bars along the Parelona road where prices would be less unreasonable than on the front. In Bar Rico, a place of chrome and saucy posters, four men were fooling around, trying to gain the attention of the three young women on barstools who were doing their best to show bored disinterest. He said loudly: 'Is any of you Francisco Ferriol?'

They stopped their shoving, shouting, and laughing, and stared aggressively at him.

'What's it to you?' one of them finally demanded.

'Cuerpo General de Policia.'

They were not frightened, as they would have been in the years when authority was challenged only by a brave man or a fool, but three of them showed a sense of caution by moving slightly away from the fourth.

'You're Ferriol,' Alvarez said as a statement, not a question. 'I'd like a word.'

'What about?'

'Will you have a drink?'

The question perplexed and worried Ferriol because the last thing he'd expected had been a friendly gesture. He looked to his companions for help; they looked away.

Alvarez crossed to the bar. 'I'll have a coñac,' he said to the bartender. 'With ice.'

The three hurriedly said they'd be seeing Ferriol sometime and left. The young women waited long enough to prove their continuing disinterest, then followed.

'Are you sure you don't want anything?' Alvarez asked.

43

'You can give us a whisky if you want,' Ferriol muttered.

His manners matched his appearance, Alvarez decided. Why did modern youth enjoy hairstyles which made them look as if they were suffering from alopecia? The barman put two glasses in front of him. 'How much?' he asked. The barman hesitated, decided discretion before profit and charged less than he would normally have done.

He carried the glasses over to one of the tables, sat. Ferriol, trying to project a sense of challenge, waited before joining him. 'What is it, then?' he asked as he sat.

'Why do I want to talk? I'm interested in last night when you were with your novia.'

'She's not my novia.'

'She seems to think she is.'

'Can't help what she thinks.'

Alvarez's dislike for the other grew. Perhaps it would be kind to let Inés know that the relationship was much less firm than she obviously thought? The idea had only to be considered to know it was ridiculous. The man who stood in the middle of a herd was liable to be struck on both sides. 'Last night, you were with Inés and you drove up to Son Fuyell and parked amongst the pine trees just inside the gates.'

'Who says?'

'She does.'

'Silly bitch!'

'I'm very old-fashioned,' Alvarez said quietly, 'so when I hear a man call a young lady a bitch, I suffer the urge to drag him along to somewhere quiet and teach him some manners.'

'You and who else?'

'A couple of friends who enjoy body-building and weight-lifting.'

Ferriol said sullenly: 'She shouldn't have told you.'

'Why not?'

'When I'm out with her, her dad thinks we're with friends.'

Alvarez would have condemned such deceit had he not been able to remember how Juana-María had, without actually lying, allowed her parents to assume she and he had been at one of her friends' homes . . . Not that in those days deceit had covered up anything more than a few kisses, sweeter than honey for having been stolen . . .

Ferriol said, less belligerently than intended: 'Why are you going on about this?'

Alvarez jerked his mind back to the present. 'While you were there, did anything unusual happen?'

'No.'

'You didn't see a car being driven very quickly on the track down from the house?'

'You meant . . . Yeah, there was a car.'

'Tell me about it.'

'There ain't nothing to tell except the driver was crazy or it was a hire car and he didn't care what happened to it.'

'Are you saying that you could see the driver was a man?'

'Yeah.'

'Would you recognize him?'

'Wouldn't reckon so.'

'But you are sure it was a man?'

'Ain't I just said?'

'Can you identify what make and type of car it was?'

'One of the new Astras – a shooting brake.'

'You seem very certain.'

'I work in a garage, don't I? I know my cars.'

'Have you any idea of its colour?'

'It was dark. Can't say no more.'

'When it reached the road, it turned left?'

'It wasn't going to turn right when that don't lead to anywhere.'

'What time was this?'

'I wasn't looking at my watch.'

'You'll know near enough.'

Ferriol finished his drink. 'Must've been around eleven. We was back at her place by midnight because if she's any later, her dad makes a bloody stupid fuss.'

Dr Sanz estimated the time of death at between seven and nine, Susana's evidence strongly suggested that Zavala had died between seven-thirty and eight. If the car was leaving

45

the property at eleven, it seemed unlikely – from the point of view of time – to have been in any way directly connected with the death. Yet the fact that it was being driven recklessly suggested a sense of panic. Had the driver waited until well after dark to leave in the expectation of doing so unobserved and the waiting had unnerved him?

On the drive to his office, Alvarez decided to phone on his arrival. In his office, it occurred to him that if Salas were late to work that morning, he would not be best pleased to have this fact exposed; better to leave the call until later. He left it until after merienda, at which point he could think of no valid reason for further delay.

The secretary with the plum-filled voice curtly told him the superior chief was at an important meeting that could not be interrupted. Typically, she cut the connection without bothering to say goodbye.

Alvarez lit a cigarette, then remembered it was only a couple of days since he'd promised himself to cut right back on smoking and drinking. He blamed his memory, not his willpower.

Salas rang at a quarter to twelve, his greeting as abrupt as ever. 'Where's your report on the Zavala case?'

'I haven't sent it yet because –'

'Of an inability to display even a basic degree of efficiency. Why did you ask for a PM?'

'Dr Sanz said that in the circumstances one would be necessary . . .'

'What are the facts of the case?'

'It's difficult to say right now –'

'Because you are the investigating officer?'

Alvarez tried to explain the problems.

'You really think that if this was not an accident, the murderer would have stayed until after dark before leaving?'

'There are two other possibilities which could just about fit the facts.'

'Name them.'

'The driver called to see Zavala, found him drowned in the pool and panicked . . .'

'Someone drove there that late at night?'

'That is one problem. Another is, if completely innocent, wouldn't he have alerted someone either immediately, or after his initial panic had subsided?'

'You talked about two possibilities.'

'The driver wasn't in a panic, but a rage. He had turned into the track leading up to Son Fuyell believing it gave access to somewhere else – despite the name on each gatepost – discovered his error, turned – which he could only have done with considerable difficulty – and returned to the road, furious at the time wasted. Drink may have muddled his mind.'

'Very likely, if a foreigner. Am I not correct in thinking that despite the ambiguous evidence of this car, you cannot say with any certainty that death was not from accidental drowning?'

'The doctor thought the blow to the head would not have been sufficient to render Zavala unconscious. And why did he fall on to the chair?'

'You have never stumbled?'

'Well, yes, but . . . If he was dazed, when he fell in he would have struggled not to drown; all he had to do was stand up because opposite the fallen chair the water would only have come up to his waist.'

'Dazed, might he not have stumbled this way and that and ended up falling in at the deep end?'

'I suppose so . . .'

'And, being a foreigner, it will almost certainly be determined that he was drunk at the time of his death. Drunken men have drowned in puddles. So to return to what I said a moment ago, you can offer no evidence to negate the probability that this was an accidental drowning?'

'A clever murderer always tries to make death look like an accident.'

'I am tempted to observe that to try to make an accident look like a murder clearly calls for something less than a clever mind.' He cut the connection.

Alvarez replaced the receiver. For the past minutes, Salas had been virtually suggesting there was no cause for further investigation. He had been arguing that there was. Such a reversal of roles normally held was very confusing.

CHAPTER 8

Alvarez slightly altered the angle of the fan in the hope that this would bring greater relief from the heat, settled back in the chair. In a perfect world, criminals would go on holiday between May and October . . .

The ringing of the telephone awoke him with a start. He wondered who could be such an insensitive fool as to interrupt his siesta? Then he realized he was in the office and it was still morning . . .

The caller was an assistant at the Institute of Forensic Anatomy. Zavala had died from drowning in fresh water. The blow to the head had not fractured the skull; it was difficult to be certain to what extent he had been affected by it, but it was possible he had been sufficiently dazed as not to be in full control of his limbs. There was one further point. On his throat was a bruise, not visible on the epidermis; connective tissues had been crushed and capillaries and smaller veins torn.

'Does that mean a really hard blow?' Alvarez asked.

'It would have been reasonably forceful. But I can't be more precise than that because different people bruise differently from the same force.'

'Have you any idea what could have caused it?'

'The shape of a bruise often can't give any indication of the object responsible and that's the case here.'

'You wouldn't like to have a guess?'

'Only a vague one and on condition I'm not quoted. It's more likely to have been something with an irregular surface, like a hand, than a regular one, like a cosh.'

'You're saying it probably was a blow from a fist?'

'Give you blokes so much as a hint and you're shouting

fact! I'm not saying anything of the sort. It might have been a fist, it might have been a hundred and one other things.'

'When did he get the bruise?'

'Close to the time of death. But if you're going to ask how close, the answer is, we can't say. When injuries occur about then, it's usually impossible to be certain.'

'Can't you be more definite about something?'

'He's dead. I know that for sure because he never said "ouch" when I started slicing.'

Alvarez mentally winced. Medical men had a sense of humour that lacked any consideration for people's susceptibilities.

'Finally, his blood to alcohol level shows he'd been drinking.'

'Could that mean he was too far gone to save himself from drowning?'

'Unless he was unusually responsive to alcohol, no.'

After the call was over, Alvarez very reluctantly came to the conclusion that he would have to phone Palma.

Salas was at his curtest. 'Yes?'

'I have just heard from the Institute, re the Zavala case, señor. Death was by drowning in fresh water; the blow to his head did not fracture his skull, but probably left him dazed, adding to the effects of the alcohol.'

'As I suggested, when he fell into the pool, he lacked the sense to save himself from drowning.'

'It seems not, señor.'

'Why not?'

'He had not been drinking that heavily. So he would surely have acted positively when he fell unless, to quote the Institute, he was peculiarly susceptible to the effects of alcohol.'

'Was he?'

'I can't say.'

'It hadn't occurred to you to find out? Is there anything more?'

'The postmortem exposed a bruise to the throat. It can't be said with any certainty what caused this, but was more likely to have been something like a fist than a cosh. It's impossible

50

to suggest when the blow was delivered beyond the fact that it would have been close to the time of death.'

'I cannot remember a previous report in which the investigating officer has been so uncertain of the facts.'

'That is the Institute's responsibility, not mine. But even as things are, we now have the probability that Zavala received a blow to the throat which caused him to fall and strike his head on the chair. I think we must now definitely treat this case as one of manslaughter or murder . . .'

'Which, in view of the evidence, you should have been doing.'

'Señor, it was you who said earlier –'

Salas cut the connection.

Alvarez altered the direction of the fan yet again. Sweet Mary! if it became any hotter, all life must stop . . . He settled back in the chair. Had Zavala been murdered or had he died in an accident? The answer, as so often, was probably to be found in a further question – Was there someone who had a motive for killing him?

Could one suspect be the owner of the car Ferriol had seen? He'd identified it as a new Astra shooting brake, dark-coloured. To try to trace it from so broad a description might seem to be as unrewarding a task as to identify a particular grain of sand on a beach. But until recently, shooting brakes had been few because popular regard had associated them with hearses, and even if that no longer held good and they had become more popular, they still could not be called common. If a list of new, dark-coloured Astra shooting brakes was drawn up, it might just be possible to identify an owner who had known Zavala . . .

Could Karen be the key to motive? An attractive woman who had tried to hide the fact she was married. The English lived strange lives, but it seemed reasonable to suppose that there were husbands who would bitterly resent the fact that they were being cuckolded. Karen was not, as far as he could judge, a very common name so the records of women of that name who held residencias could be searched; photographs could then be shown to Susana . . .

51

He congratulated himself. By using logic, he had found how to proceed with the case at no immediate cost of effort to himself. Then he remembered that he had not yet had a word with Lorenzo . . .

A phone call to Susana at Son Fuyell had determined Lorenzo had not turned up for work that morning, so Alvarez waited until after his siesta before driving to the other's home.

The finca was almost halfway between Cardona and the coast. The unrestored farmhouse – a rarity after the invasion of the foreigners – was surrounded by open farmland. He stepped out of his car and enjoyed the breadth of space, watching a hovering kestrel that suddenly glided away and out of sight, listening to the distant clanging of sheep bells. It obviously was not the best land – the soil was a light grey, stony, and at irregular intervals great slabs of rock reached up out of it – but he would have traded almost all he possessed for the chance to be able to walk into the centre of one of the fields and know it was his . . .

A man sidled around the corner of the house, his expression vacuous. He was silent. What wasn't said, couldn't harm.

'Are you Lorenzo Frau?' Alvarez asked.

'Who wants to know?'

'I'm Enrique Alvarez, Cuerpo General de Policia.'

Frau cleared his throat.

'I phoned Son Fuyell and they told me that although you work mornings there, you didn't turn up today.'

'Damaged me leg last night.' Frau hurriedly massaged his right thigh. 'Otherwise I'd have been up there, doing the garden, even if there's no saying who'll be paying.'

A dog appeared, long tail held low because it was uncertain how it would be received. It hesitated, then barked at Alvarez.

'Shut up,' Frau shouted, glad to be able to vent his uneasiness.

The dog backed away and began to pant.

Silence returned. Frau, realizing he was faced by someone as stubborn as he, became more uneasy by the second. Finally, he said hoarsely: 'What are you after?'

Even now, after he'd forced the other off balance, Alvarez knew that to approach the reason for his visit too abruptly would be to learn nothing. 'You've a nice place here.'

'The land's so poor it ain't worth a peseta a hectare.'

'There's many a German would pay you much more than one peseta.'

'I ain't selling.'

'How many hectares are there?'

The question raised in Frau's mind the frightening possibility that he was about to be questioned over the amount of income he declared to the tax authorities. 'I don't know.'

'So many you've never found the energy to count them?'

'There's just under seven, that's all.' Only after speaking did he realize he'd been tricked into making nonsense of his previous denial. Momentarily, his expression of blank stupidity faltered.

Satisfied he'd gained the psychological high ground, Alvarez said: 'It's too hot out here in the sun. Suppose we move before you tell me what I want to hear?'

'I don't know nothing about anything,' was Frau's weak riposte. Very reluctantly, he led the way into the house.

The front room had no glass in the window – only a wooden shutter – and the floor was hard-packed earth. Hanging on the walls were several faded, framed photographs of stern-faced men and women wearing Sunday suits and traditional dresses; against the walls were half a dozen chairs, no two of which were of the same pattern; in the centre was a polished brass cauldron in which was a large aspidistra. The lack of any comfort or grace could have been taken as a sign of poverty; Alvarez knew it identified Frau as someone who remembered that to live richly was to die poor.

Frau struggled to work out whether he'd anything to gain by offering hospitality. He came to the conclusion he'd nothing to lose. 'Juana,' he shouted.

A woman, dressed in nondescript, heavily worn, but very clean clothes, her skin darkened and leathered by the hours spent in the fields, came through the inner doorway. 'Get some wine,' he ordered. She turned and left.

The dog appeared in the outside doorway, then vanished when Frau cursed it and made as if to throw something. They waited, letting time slide past.

The woman returned with an earthenware jug of wine and two glasses which she put down on the ground by Frau's chair, left, again without speaking.

'Have you been working long at Son Fuyell?' Alvarez asked.

'Can't remember.'

'Were you there when the previous owner was alive?'

'Couldn't say.'

'It'll be easy enough to find out.'

Frau said hoarsely: 'Why are you asking?'

'To find out if you've known Señor Zavala long enough to tell me what kind of man he was.'

Frau worked on his lower lip with his four remaining front teeth. 'Is that what you're after? Because of him dying in the pool?'

'Why else would I be here?'

That was a question he certainly was not going to answer. But his relief was made clear by the alacrity with which he filled the two glasses and even stood to pass one to Alvarez.

The wine was very rough, had an earthy taste, and would have made a connoisseur spit immediately. Alvarez drank it with pleasure because it reminded him of the past when his parents had been alive and life had been so hard that even a glass of wine had been counted a luxury. 'What did you think of the señor?'

'How d'you mean?'

'What kind of man did you think him?'

Frau was very willing to list someone else's faults, even if he found it difficult to put into words exactly what he wanted to say. Zavala had been arrogant, rude, and incredibly ill-mannered; a gypsy from Andalucia would have behaved with more dignity. He'd been stupid – thought he spoke good Castilian when it was South American argot. He'd treated the staff as if they were slaves, demanding they work themselves into their graves for a mere pittance. When he'd been asked

54

for a new hedge-cutter to replace the one that was always breaking down, he'd said that he couldn't afford it. 'They're all the same, the richer, the meaner.'

'Maybe that's because they've more to lose.'

'And temper! Do something he didn't like and he was shouting himself red in the face. Like the time Santiago and him were going on at each other. It got so as I thought maybe only one of 'em would be eating supper.'

'Who's Santiago?'

'A local builder.'

'What was the row about?'

'The work he'd been doing. The señor said it hadn't been done properly. Bloody fool! Everyone knows Santiago is the best builder in the area.'

'When was this – recently?'

'The oranges was ripe 'cause I was picking 'em for the house and carrying 'em up when I heard 'em at it. Good oranges, only he said they wasn't as sweet as they ought to have been. As if he'd know!'

'Then it was in January or February?'

'You think oranges ripen in July?'

Alvarez drained his glass. 'This is really good.'

'You've the looks of someone who finds other people's wine is always good.' Alcohol went quickly to Frau's tongue and he had half forgotten the need for caution. He stood, picked up the jug, refilled both their glasses.

'They tell me the señor was fond of the ladies,' Alvarez observed.

'Couldn't live without 'em, lucky sod.'

'And recently he's been seeing a lot of one in particular?'

Frau sniggered. 'I reckon I've seen near as much of her as he has.'

'What's that – wishful thinking?'

'I know what I see. I was working down the south side of the property, clearing some land, and had to come back for a handbill. Know what I saw?'

'Tell me.'

'When I came past the pool, there was a lot of laughing, so I . . .'

'Had a look to see what was going on?'

'I wanted to see they wasn't trespassers, using the señor's pool without permission.'

'Very commendable of you.'

'They always say you lot from Llueso are sarcastic bastards.'

'We need something to be in our favour. What did you see?'

'Him and her and not so much as a handkerchief on 'em. How about that?'

'People often strip off when they're sunbathing and don't expect anyone to be around.'

'They wasn't sunbathing.'

'Are you saying they were active?'

'Well, not exactly,' Frau said reluctantly. 'But they had been just before I got there.'

'The vibes were still vibrating?'

'I've eyes. And doesn't a ram tup a ewe whenever it gets the chance?' Frau finished his drink, poured what was left in the jug into his glass, drank.

'You're sure you're not making all the better parts up?' Alvarez asked.

'You calling me a liar?'

'Could be an optimist. It's unusual for people to carry on like that if there's a risk of being seen.'

'Then they was unusual. But if you don't believe me, ask her if she don't have a funny-looking birthmark on her bum.'

'A difficult question to put delicately.'

'I'm telling you, she's not keen on delicacy!'

'Susana, or Inés, told me that when she's gone to Son Fuyell, she's been driven there by a man. Can't be her husband, so who is he?'

'How would I know? Tell you something, though. If he was lying by the pool with a dozen women starkers, none of 'em would get so much as tickled.'

'How old would you say he is?'

'Near enough her age.'

It was difficult to surmise what part in the triangle he could play.

Frau went to refill his glass, found the jug empty. 'Juana,' he shouted.

Alvarez settled back in the chair.

CHAPTER 9

Five photostat copies of residencias were faxed to Alvarez on Monday morning. Two of the women were in their seventies, two in their sixties; the fifth was in her twenties, and if one allowed for the poor quality of the reproduction it was clear she would quicken an anchorite's heart. Someone in Palma had shown initiative and enclosed very brief biographical notes and from these he learned that Karen Robertson was married to a man of fifty-six. Even for a homely woman, a thirty-year difference in ages was likely to strain marriage loyalties; for a voluptuously attractive one, it could be all but guaranteed to snap them. He was confident he had identified Zavala's companion by the swimming pool.

As Alvarez stepped out of his car in the turning circle in front of Son Fuyell and once again took the time to enjoy the view, a pleasure heightened by the slight breeze that always seemed to blow over high ground, he experienced a rare jealousy. Why should one man be granted so much? . . . Yet in truth Zavala had been granted an early, watery death. There were those who claimed that life was always fairer than it might at first appear to be.

Inés, no longer emotional, let him into the house. After telling him Susana had driven down to the village but would almost certainly be back soon, she suggested he might like some coffee. In the kitchen, she asked him if he knew what was going to happen to the house. Would she and Susana be asked to stay on? She hoped they would because she was saving for when she and Francisco married. Everywhere these days cost an absolute fortune. There was a house in the village, not far from her parents, and the owner was asking sixteen million for it. Sixteen million! Years ago, one could have bought the whole village for that! Maybe they'd have to rent somewhere to begin with, but rents were so very high . . .

He listened to her prattle, sadly certain that only unhappiness lay ahead of her – either Francisco would marry her or he wouldn't.

The coffee machine hissed. She poured out two mugfuls, put milk and sugar on the table, and sat. Why were parents so stupid? Last night, she and Francisco had gone for a drive and returned a little latish and her father had worked himself into a temper and accused her of . . . Well, of misbehaving. She wasn't that kind of a girl. She looked quickly at him.

He assured her that it was obvious she was not that kind of a girl.

They heard a car door slam. 'That'll be Susana.' She left the kitchen.

Alvarez drank and his mind wandered in the past. In June – or had it been July? – Juana-María had said she'd wanted to go on a picnic. Her parents, who had never understood her liking for new experiences, had been bewildered by the wish because it was not something they, or any of their friends, had ever done, but in the end they'd agreed – naturally, provided a duenna accompanied them. It had been a day of sunshine, laughter, and happiness; he could still recall his exalted certainty that the world had nothing more wonderful to offer. He should have realized that to believe one had reached a peak was to accept that the only way forward was down. It hadn't been long afterwards that Juana-María had died, pinned against a wall by a car driven by a drunken Frenchman . . .

Inés returned, accompanied by Susana who poured out for herself what coffee remained. He produced the photocopy of Karen's residencia and passed it across. 'Do you recognize her?' he asked Susana.

She held it well away from her face, then opened her handbag and brought out a case from which she took a pair of spectacles. She put them on and examined the photograph a second time. 'That's her. She's married, isn't she?'

'She is.'

'But not to the man who drove her here?'

'No.'

'So who's he?'

'I don't yet know, but I expect I'll find out.'

Susana finished her coffee. 'You reckon the señor definitely didn't drown accidentally, don't you?'

'I don't yet know whether he did or not.'

She turned to Inés. 'If that's the case, you'd better tell him about the glass.'

'He won't want to hear about that,' she said scathingly. 'Her friend drives one of those lovely BMWs. Francisco says it'll do two hundred and fifty kilometres an hour. Just imagine!'

'It's ridiculous to go so fast.'

Inés giggled. 'Lorenzo says you drive so slowly that you don't even do sixty downhill.'

'I think of other people.'

Alvarez intervened in what appeared to be a long-running argument. 'What is there to tell me about a glass?'

'It's nothing,' Inés answered. 'You wouldn't be interested.'

'Until I hear what this is about, I won't know if that's right.'

'It's just that one went missing.'

'A glass?'

'Yes.'

'From where and when?'

'I went down Friday to tidy up around the pool 'cause Susana said to do it – I couldn't think why since the señor wasn't there to fuss any more . . .'

'Show some respect,' Susana snapped.

Alvarez said peacefully: 'And what happened when you tidied things up?'

'Like always, I checked the glass cupboard and there was two glasses missing. You'd said you'd taken one to look at it, or something, but there wasn't no sign of the other. That's all. Like as not, the señor had dropped it and broke it before he died.'

'Then he'd have told us to clear up the mess,' Susana said. 'And even if for once he'd done something for himself, where was all the broken glass?'

'How sure are you that there's one unaccounted for?' he asked.

'Positive,' Inés answered.

'When was the last time you knew all the glasses were there?'

'I don't know. The last time I looked, I suppose.'

'When would that have been?'

'The day he died. I had to clean and tidy the poolhouse every morning, even if he didn't have visitors. Never met anyone so fussy.'

'And every morning, you checked the contents of the glass cupboard?'

'If something wasn't in its right place, he'd start shouting. He'd a terrible temper and he could become real nasty.'

'You shouldn't speak like that of someone who's died,' Susana said.

'I speak as I find.'

Alvarez wondered how much of Inés's sharp criticism had its roots in the incident in the library.

Inés said: 'It don't signify, does it? Just a missing glass.'

'I'm not so certain.' He saw Susana's quick smile of satisfaction at his answer . . . Inés could be mistaken and one glass had been missing for some time and despite all her certainty, she'd not noticed that fact; it was there, but not in its right place; she might have broken it and was using the present story to cover that fact; she might have the times mixed up and it had not gone missing after Tuesday morning . . . But if she was correct then there had to be the possibility that a second person had been drinking with Zavala and that he had removed his glass, on which would be prints, to hide the fact that anyone else had been present. Yet if a murderer could think that clearly and had been calm enough to wait until dark to drive away, why had he appeared to be in a panic? Because a man could

61

suddenly, inexplicably, be overcome by a fear so great that he virtually lost all self-control? He broke a silence which, he realized from their expressions, had lasted a considerable time. 'Inés, I'd like you to come down to the poolhouse to make certain that one glass is missing and not just misplaced.'

'I've told you, haven't I?' she said resentfully.

He smiled. 'In my job, everything has to be checked a dozen times. I even have to look in the mirror each morning to make certain it's me.' She did not find that amusing and on brief reflection, he agreed with her.

Inés had too butterfly a nature to harbour casual resentment and by the time she and Alvarez reached the pool, she was once more chatting cheerfully.

When he examined the glass cupboard, at the back of the main area in the poolhouse, he accepted that it was obvious if a glass were missing – the different types were in regimented blocks, each carefully separated from the next. On the top shelf were a number of shapely tumblers, of the same pattern as the one he'd taken away. The front row lacked two. 'They were all here the last time you checked before the señor died and that was Tuesday morning?'

She sighed. 'Isn't that what I keep saying?'

He thanked her for her help and suggested she returned to the house. Rather reluctantly, she did so.

Having searched the area once, logically a second search would be a waste of time. An assumption very welcome in such heat. Yet, irritatingly, he found it impossible to strangle the thought that he should make one.

Because the skimming net was in full sunlight, which it had not been the previous Tuesday, he noticed that in it were several hairs, almost certainly human. There seemed to be too many for them to be part of the normal detritus one could expect to find in a pool and he visually examined them carefully. Some had their roots. Not shed naturally, but pulled out by force? . . .

He pictured Zavala, unbalanced by a blow to the throat, falling on to the patio chair and from there collapsing into the pool; the second man using the skimming net to entangle his head and hold it under the water until he drowned . . .

He collected up the hairs and, lacking anything else, put them in one of the glasses from the cupboard.

CHAPTER 10

Estart Caves, a kilometre to the east of the village, had been discovered many years before by a shepherd searching for a lost lamb. Initially, they'd been used for hiding contraband, but when the tourists started to arrive in ever increasing numbers, a villager who'd inherited his business acumen from his Catalan father, had realized their potential as an attraction and had bought the hill. He enlarged the entrance, provided rough footways that were relatively safe, and bribed tour operators and bus drivers to direct the tourists to them. They became reasonably popular, but reasonable profit could never satisfy a Catalan. Something had to be done to increase their popularity. He named several stalactites after angels and groups of stalagmites after noted biblical scenes, reasoning that people would experience what they were told they were experiencing, else why would studio audiences laugh at TV comedy shows? He was proved correct. The number of visitors rose and there were a few amongst them who swore they'd seen stalactites quiver.

Ca'n Jerome, sited on a low roll of land, overlooked at a distance the entrance to the caves, now marked by a large car and bus park, memento shop, café, and the vivid colours of the bougainvillaea which had been planted around the area. Alvarez climbed out of his car and stared across at the many parked vehicles. They represented the wealth brought by tourism, the rape of the island by the tourists. As the foreigner's habit of calling houses by their own names represented a denial of island customs – houses had been called by nicknames, not Christian names, often critical or amusingly rude.

He crossed to the front door and rang the bell. The door

64

was opened by a woman, not yet thirty but whose features were already beginning to coarsen. 'Are Señor and Señora Robertson here?' he asked.

'The señor is, but the señora is out,' Dominica answered.

He introduced himself.

'You'd best come in,' she said uncertainly. Alvarez stepped into the hall and she closed the door. 'The señor's not very well this evening.'

'I'm sorry to hear that – what's the trouble?'

She shrugged her shoulders.

He followed her into the sitting room, cool thanks to the air-conditioning. Robertson was watching television and when he looked up, he did not try to hide his irritation. 'What is it?' he demanded in English.

She tried to answer, but he could not understand her.

'Señor,' Alvarez said, having to raise his voice to overcome the television, 'I should like to speak with you.'

'Who the devil are you?'

'Inspector Alvarez, Cuerpo General de Policia.'

'The police?'

'That is correct.'

'What d'you want with me?'

The English had a saying, Politeness costs nothing. Perhaps that was why some of them didn't value it. 'May I sit down and explain?'

'If you must.'

As he sat, Dominica left. 'I gather you're not very well, señor. I hope you are not suffering from anything serious?'

'God knows. The local doctors are incapable of finding out.'

'Perhaps if you saw a specialist in Palma?'

'Just as incompetent.'

There was clearly no point in any further sympathetic interest. 'No doubt you have heard of the tragic death of Señor Zavala, who lived in Cardona?'

'What about that?'

'When such an incident occurs, it is of course necessary to try to find out why. That is what I'm doing.'

'Then there's no call to bother me.'

'But I understand that you and your wife knew him.'

'What's that?'

'Señor, do you think the television might go off?'

'This is a wonderful country! A stranger comes in and tells you what to do in your own house!'

'It would help us to hear each other more easily.'

Robertson muttered bad-temperedly as he used the remote control to switch off the television.

'Thank you, señor . . . Did you and your wife know Señor Zavala?'

'What if we did?'

'Then you may be able to help me.'

Robertson opened a chased silver box and brought out a cigarette, lit this with a silver lighter embossed with a crest.

'When did you last see Señor Zavala?'

'A couple of weeks ago. He invited us to dinner. Typically, right over the top and too much of everything. You'd never think from his behaviour he'd been a diplomat, even if that was for a tin-pot country.'

'In what capacity did he serve?'

'No idea. Doorman, judging by the way he behaved, but to listen to him you'd think he ran the country.'

'When did he retire?'

'Couldn't say.'

'Perhaps you did not like him very much?'

'We English observe standards. A gentleman does not try to impress.'

'For fear of giving the wrong impression?'

'What's that? Are you trying to be smart?'

'Of course not, señor.'

'Then you'd better learn to speak better English.' He stubbed out the cigarette, stood, crossed to the small bar that was a feature of the large sitting room and poured out a whisky, added soda, opened an ice container. 'Not again!' He reached over to the wall to press a bell and when Dominica entered, said: 'Why the devil can't you do your job properly? You've forgotten the ice.'

She clearly had not understood him.

Alvarez said in Mallorquin: 'He's asking you if you'd be kind enough to get some ice, please.'

'Yes? When he thinks himself such a hidalgo he wouldn't say please to God?' She left.

'What was she saying?' Robertson demanded.

'She was apologizing for not having seen there was no ice.'

'They're all incompetent.'

She returned and put a second ice container on the bar, left. Robertson helped himself to two cubes of ice, crossed to his chair, sat.

No Mallorquin would ever drink in front of a fellow human without having asked what he would like; English manners were indeed different. 'From what you said earlier, señor, you did not regard Señor Zavala as a close friend?'

'I don't see it's any of your business how I regarded him.'

'Whilst the drowning seems to have been accidental, it is possible it was not.'

'You're saying he may have been murdered? That's why you're asking impertinent questions? If you're suggesting I could have had anything to do with his death, I'll damned well sue you for slander.'

'I'm asking questions to try to find out more about the man Señor Zavala was because if I can succeed, I may learn if there was someone who could have wished him dead.'

'You go about things a bloody funny way! Still, that's hardly surprising in this country.'

'Do you know when the señora will return?'

'Why's that any concern of yours?'

'I wish to speak with her.'

'There's no need for that.'

'I'm afraid I must be the judge.'

'Do I know I'm living in Spain! You burst into my house and try to order me around, then tell me you'll decide what happens in it!'

Alvarez stood. 'Will you please tell the señora that I will need to speak to her in the near future, so perhaps she will be kind enough to get in touch with me at the post in Llueso and say when would be most convenient to her.'

'You obviously haven't understood a word I've said.'

'That is possible. But as Jaime Borras wrote, To misunderstand is the first step to understanding.' He said a polite goodbye and was unsurprised when there was no response.

He made his way out of the cool of the house and settled behind the wheel of his car which, having been standing in the sun, was like an oven. As he drove on to the road, he tried to reach behind the ill-mannered, pompous xenophobia and judge whether he had spoken to the man or his mask.

Because he had arrived home late – so late there had been time for only one drink before Dolores served lunch – he had enjoyed a longer than usual siesta and it was nearly six before he returned to the office. Almost immediately, the phone rang. The caller, who worked in Vehicles, complained that he'd wasted the entire afternoon trying to get through. As Alvarez explained that work had kept him out of the building until then, he reflected that it was the tourists who had brought to the island an unwanted sense of urgency.

'What's more, your request has been a bloody nuisance! The computer wasn't programmed to handle it and trying to make it cope caused it to crash . . .'

He listened, understanding perhaps one word in six. How much time and frustration would be saved if man relearned the art of keeping records with pen and paper?

Eventually, the caller said: 'Anyway, thanks to my genius, I finally managed to persuade it to spit out a list of new, dark-coloured Astra shooting brakes; d'you want me to fax it?'

'Are there many cars?'

'Enough to keep you out of mischief for a while.'

'Then perhaps you'll also extract the names and addresses of any foreign owners and add them to the list before you fax it.'

'You think I've nothing else to do?'

Alvarez said goodbye. There were some who were seldom

eager to help others if this meant any inconvenience to themselves.

The list of cars was dauntingly long, proving how the popularity of shooting brakes had suddenly increased. However, only three were owned by foreigners who lived in the area. If the gods were kind, the driver of the car seen on the Tuesday would prove to be one of the three.

CHAPTER 11

As Alvarez drove carefully around the right-angled bend in the dirt track, Ca'n Liodre came in sight above the tops of the orange trees – the grove was on land a couple of metres lower. An old farmhouse, reformed for a Mallorquin owner, he judged – the windows had not been enlarged.

He parked in front of the lean-to garage in which was a dark-green Astra shooting brake, its numberplate showing it to be only months old. He left his car and walked across the badly laid concrete above which, on a rusty trellis, grew an ancient vine that was laden with bunches of grapes that would soon be ripe.

The original wooden door, grey and pitted with age, had been swung back against the stone wall; inset were two modern wooden and glass doors. He knocked and when there was no answer, knocked again. Finally, he stepped inside – something he would have done immediately if Mallorquins had been living there – and called out. As he waited, he looked around himself. Originally the main room of the house with a very large, cowled fireplace around which the family would have sat in the winter, now the area was a hall and contained no more than a couple of leather-backed chairs, three framed photographs of Llueso in the past century on one wall and a small, crudely fashioned hanging on another.

There were the sounds of shoes on bare tiles and then a man came through the doorway immediately to the side of the open staircase. Alvarez introduced himself.

'Come on through.'

Beyond the doorway was what had originally been a barn; the crudely beamed ceiling was five metres high at its apex and there was a small gallery. Thanks to the height, the very thick rock walls, and the single small window, the sitting room was cool – it was also so dimly lit that even in the height of summer, the overhead cluster of lights was switched on.

'Take a seat.' Bailey gestured with his hand in the general direction of three chairs and a settee, none of which was of matching design or covered in matching material – landlords had long since learned not to cosset foreign tenants. 'Can I offer you a drink?'

A different character from Robertson! 'Thank you, señor. If I might have a coñac with only ice?'

Bailey went through a second doorway into the kitchen – as Alvarez was able to judge since the door was left open. Bailey returned with a tray on which were bottles, two glasses, ice, and a lemon. As he put the tray down, a woman entered through the first doorway. He quickly turned. 'What is it?'

'I'm joining you for a drink, of course . . . Are you going to introduce me?'

He hesitated, then said abruptly: 'My wife, Fenella. Inspector Alvarez.'

No great beauty, Alvarez thought, but lucky possessor of something almost as quickly discernible and of far greater value – the quality of warmth. He was glad he had shaved and put on a clean shirt.

Bailey spoke to his wife. 'You're obviously forgetting you're due at the coffee morning in aid of the local dogs' home.'

'That's tomorrow.'

'Today. So you'll have to make your excuses and miss a drink.'

She hesitated, then left the room.

'Women,' Bailey said, 'have a good sense of time, but not of dates.'

She returned, a small book in her hand. 'And men should learn to look before they correct.' She went up to where he stood and held the book open. 'Tomorrow. A public *mea culpa*, please.'

Bailey, his expression annoyed, shrugged his shoulders.

'If that's not to be forthcoming, I'll accept a G and T instead.' She turned to Alvarez. 'Harry says you're a detective?'

'Yes, I am, señora.'

'Are you here because we have unwittingly done something terrible?'

'I need to ask a few questions,' he answered evasively.

'About what?'

Bailey said: 'There's no need to worry –'

She interrupted him. 'I'm not worrying, just curious.'

'And you know what curiosity does.'

'I hope you don't equate me with a cat?'

'Only in feline grace.'

'Very laboured.'

'But some marks for intention? . . . I'll get another glass.'

A couple so at ease that they could be quite rude to each other, knowing their words would be accepted humorously? Alvarez wondered. Probably . . . And yet Bailey had sounded annoyed rather than surprised when she'd first appeared and it seemed that there was an undercurrent of tension to their lightly spoken words.

Bailey poured out drinks, handed glasses around, sat. 'Now, what's the problem and how can we help?'

'Perhaps you have heard of the death of Señor Zavala?' Alvarez said.

'The bush telegraph has been working overtime. We were told about it almost as soon as it happened. Presumably, then, that's why you're here?'

'Yes, it is.'

'There's something about his drowning which raises a problem?'

'It seems possible it was not an accident.'

'Is that a euphemistic way of saying he may have been deliberately killed?'

'There is reason for believing that that may be so.'

'Good God!'

'Which is, you'll understand, why I have to ask questions of the people who may be able to help me to discover the truth.'

'Of course. But I can't think you'll find us of any use.'

'But it is correct that you knew him?'

'We met him once only, at a cocktail party.'

'When was this?'

'Ironically, on the day he died. It came as quite a shock to hear what had happened. At midday, full of life and, it has to be added, himself; that night, dead. Whoever it was said that life is more transitory than any of us dare acknowledge, knew what he was talking about.'

'Presumably, this party was given by friends of yours?'

'Friends of friends. We're still newcomers to the island and the Achesons, who've been very kind, were invited by Dolly Selby and they asked if they could take us along because they reckoned we'd have the chance to meet some of the more interesting expats, as Dolly always serves good champagne.'

'And you were introduced to Señor Zavala?'

'Much to his annoyance.'

'Why is that?'

'He was in deep conversation with a very liberated redhead – judging by her lack of dress. Unfortunately for him, Dolly is the epitome of a cocktail party hostess and she has only to see a couple enjoying each other's conversation to break up the tête-à-tête. She led the redhead away and poor Guido was left with us.'

'And you talked with him for how long?'

'Until we decided to ease his pain and move on, leaving him free to pursue the redhead.'

'You would not have had time to learn anything about him, then?'

'We learned more than enough,' Fenella said.

Alvarez turned to face her. 'From your tone, señora, it sounds as if you instinctively disliked him?'

'I –'

Bailey interrupted her. 'Nothing raises my wife's hackles more quickly than a man who obviously thinks himself irresistible and lays on the charm with a trowel. Not that she would ever describe it as charm.'

'And you, señor, how did you regard him?'

'With amusement rather than dislike, since he wasn't aiming his charm at me, and it amuses me to hear someone claiming the world wouldn't turn without his assistance.'

73

'What was he boasting about?'

'Himself. How important he'd been when in the diplomatic service, what taste in modern art he possessed, the style he brought to living – in another fifteen minutes, I don't doubt we'd have learned how he inspired his old friend Michael to paint the Sistine Chapel.'

'Did you see him again after the party?'

'Of course not.'

'Are you quite certain?'

'That's an odd question in view of what I've just said.'

'Nevertheless, I should like an answer.'

'Why? D'you really think that after leaving the party I'd immediately have rushed off to see someone I'd be happy never to meet again? If so, perhaps I'd better be more specific. We spoke to Guido Zavala for probably no more than ten minutes, but in that time both Fenella and I judged him to be someone we did not want to become friendly with – a judgement which I'm perfectly prepared to accept can reflect badly on us rather than on him. Does that answer you?'

'A car was seen leaving his home that evening, soon after dark, and it was being driven very recklessly. This raises the possibility that the driver was under an emotional strain.'

'You're suggesting the driver was responsible for Zavala's death?'

'That has to be a possibility.'

'And, since this has to be the point of your questioning, you think I was the driver . . . ?'

'That's utterly absurd,' Fenella said sharply.

Bailey spoke lightly. 'After a policeman has been dealing with the public for even a short time, I suspect that the absurd becomes commonplace.' He spoke to Alvarez. 'Isn't that so?'

'I would have used the word "unusual" instead of absurd.'

'Because it's more diplomatic?'

Alvarez smiled. 'The car has been identified as a new, dark-coloured Astra shooting brake, driven by a male. As shooting brakes are still relatively rare on this island – though rapidly becoming more popular – I have had a list drawn up of those which are owned in this area. You are one of only three foreign owners. You knew Señor Zavala.'

'From little acorns, great oak trees truly do grow! Would you think me rude if I pointed out the fallacies in your conclusion?'

'Of course not.'

'But our glasses are empty, so first let me refill them.' He stood, collected the glasses, and left.

Fenella, with a poise Alvarez admired, talked about the house they were renting and remarked, with resigned amusement, that some of the hot-water pipes had been taken around the outside of the house so that if they still lived there during the coming winter, a hot bath would be difficult . . .

Bailey returned, handed them their glasses, sat. 'I hope this won't sound too pompous, but had we wished to make further contact with Guido, I would not have felt the need to do so within only a few hours of first meeting him. According to himself, he was very rich, and such eagerness on our part would have aroused his deepest suspicions – the rich find it very difficult to separate themselves from their riches. The next point. Is it correct that he died in the evening?'

'Yes.'

'And you said that this car was seen after dark?'

'That's right.'

'Then any identification has to be very uncertain.'

'It was seen by someone who is knowledgeable about cars and there was nearly a full moon.'

'Moonlight is known to distort, as many a couple have discovered a few years into their marriage . . . Does the observer claim to be able to identify the driver?'

'No.'

'Is there any reason to be certain that the car did not come from another area of the island?'

'No.'

'Have you spoken to the other two foreign owners of similar cars?'

'Not yet.'

'So you can't be certain whether, or not, they knew Guido . . . I think, Inspector, that you've been fishing.'

'I'm no fisherman, señor, but I understand that one only fishes where there is reason to think there might be fish.'

'Touché,' said Fenella.

Bailey smiled. 'But to show what a poor catch I represent, I wasn't driving anywhere that night, I was here, with Fenella, watching television on an illegal card smuggled out from England – a confession made to convince you of my good faith and in the hopes that you will take no official action.'

'On this island, smuggling has always been regarded as a legitimate occupation.' Alvarez drained his glass. He stood. 'Thank you for your help.'

'Which can't have helped.'

'A negative can be as useful as a positive.'

As, a few minutes later, he drove away from Ca'n Liodre, question jostled question. Had Bailey been trying to persuade his wife to leave the house before the questions began? Had she been equally determined to stay to judge the situation for herself? Had this disagreement led to tension? Had his explanation of their obvious dislike of Zavala been genuine? Why had he gone to such lengths to try to prove the car seen by Francisco could not have been correctly identified, when the normal reaction would surely have been a simple flat denial that it could have been his? . . . Yet if the Baileys had not met Zavala before the cocktail party, it had to be ridiculous to suppose that in the course of a meeting lasting roughly ten minutes, Bailey could find cause to murder.

Why did life always have to be so complicated? Alvarez wondered.

CHAPTER 12

Pons's house was on the western side of Cardona, where the hills and mountains, arching northwards, formed a backdrop rather than being part of the land; the soil was light and grew peppers noted for their flavour – to tell a young woman she was as sweet as a Cardona pepper was to flatter her.

Alvarez parked his car, climbed out, and looked around him. There was a well-kept flower garden and a pond in which ornamental ducks were paddling; to the right of where he stood there was an ornate fountain, carved out of sandstone by someone with considerable skill and artistic ability; on the patio of the house were two small statues of fawns. That all this should belong to a Mallorquin was surprising since the centuries had taught the islanders what to value – a tomato plant that bore was valuable, a rose bush, no matter how many and magnificent its blooms, was not. He climbed the steps to the covered patio, crossed to the front door, opened this and stepped into a room that was furnished in a style only partly Mallorquin. Clearly, there was a foreign influence here. He called out.

Rosa came through a doorway, stopped, and stared at him, her brown eyes filled with curiosity.

He smiled at her. 'Hullo. I'm Enrique. Who are you?'

'Rosa.'

'That's a pretty name.'

'I know it is.'

'Is your father here?'

'Yes.'

'Would you tell him I'm here and would like a word with him.'

She left. He moved to stare at a large framed photograph,

hanging on the wall, of a young girl, sufficiently like Rosa to identify her as a sister, who was taking part in the Festa de L'Estendard and was dressed in white with the carefully modelled body of a heavily caparisoned horse around her waist. It did a man's heart good to know that the old traditions were being continued, despite the tourists . . . Or was it, in truth, because of the tourists? Was it their malign money which kept them going . . . ?

'Who are you?'

He'd been so deep in thought that he had not heard Pons's approach. He introduced himself to a man who carried tradition on his shoulders – short, stocky, face roughened and lined, shoulders broad, manner of speech coarse and abrupt, like every peasant, challenging life even whilst knowing he must die and therefore lose the fight.

'What d'you want here?' His Mallorquin had the guttural accent that was peculiar to those who lived in, or near, Cardona.

'I'm making inquiries following the death of Sẽnor Zavala.'

'So?'

'He drowned in his swimming pool.'

'And if he did?'

'There's the question, did he do so accidentally or because someone pushed him under.'

'Why come asking me?'

'If he was murdered, someone didn't like him.'

'Must take a lot of learning to be smart enough to work that out.'

Alvarez continued to speak with the same good humour, accepting the other's bloody-minded attitude as a natural defence against authority. 'I'm wondering if you can suggest who might have disliked him?'

'Why should I be able to?'

'You did work for him.'

'Who says?'

'Are you denying you did?'

There was no answer. More people had been hanged by their tongues than their hands.

'I was told you're the best builder in the area, so he employed you since he always wanted the best.'

'But didn't bloody well want to pay for it!' Pons said with sudden, sharp bitterness.

'He owed you money?'

Pons cursed himself.

'Did he?'

'You think I give credit?'

'Not voluntarily.'

There was a long silence.

Alvarez finally said: 'I reckon the biggest bastards are the foreigners who come here and take advantage of us. They get us to do work, knowing that if things turn wrong they needn't pay what they owe because all they have to do is slip back to their own country and it'll either be impossible or not worth the effort to trace 'em. But Señor Zavala didn't time things right, so you can get the estate to settle. I'll be looking around, so if I find proof that you did work for which he never paid, I'll let you have it.'

'He's dead. There's the end to his debts.'

'That's how it used to be when debts were small and there was a widow who needed every peseta she could touch, but it's a different world now. You think anyone's going to stand out for a foreigner against one of us?'

'He said he wasn't paying because the work wasn't good enough.' Pons was almost shouting. 'All his money and he talked that crap!' He stumped his way out on to the patio, slumped down on one of the chairs that were set around a large wooden table.

Alvarez joined him. 'What work did you do?'

Zavala had wanted a bedroom, a sitting room, and a bathroom, added to a house already so large that half an army could camp in it. He'd asked for an estimate, rejected it on the grounds that the total was far too large. As if even a million pesetas made any difference to the likes of him. And, for a foreigner, it had been an honest estimate. Times weren't good. In the end, the estimate had been reduced and resubmitted and finally, after quibbling about this, that, and the other, he'd accepted it. Then, when it was time for the first payment, he'd said he'd settle when the job was completed. He – Pons – had worked along with his men and twice as hard as they from dawn to dusk; he'd worked until his hands had blistered – hands roughened by a lifetime's labour. With the job done, he'd asked for settlement. Zavala had refused to pay on the grounds that the work wasn't up to the standard promised. That had been balls! The work was first class. The bastard had been holding on to the money, like the miser he was. In desperation, he'd been asked for half the total, the rest to be paid when full agreement was reached. He'd refused; he'd said that if the company was in trouble because money had had to be paid to third parties, that was none of his concern. In desperation, an abogado had been called in to help. As much use as an empty well, but he'd wanted paying; unlike builders, lawyers were paid for being incompetent . . . Pons became silent, overcome by the iniquities of an unfair world.

Rosa came out on to the patio and said Mummy wanted to know if they'd like something to drink? Pons hesitated, but his previous antagonism towards Alvarez had been swallowed up by his hatred of the dead Zavala; he asked Alvarez what he wanted. He told Rosa to bring out a bottle of brandy and some ice.

Both men were silent. One of the ducks on the pond quacked and was answered by others; cicadas began to shrill; the ghost of a breeze stirred the bell-like flowers of a datura; a flock of pigeons swept overhead in a wide arc.

Rosa returned, concentrating very hard on the tray in her hands. She put this down on the table, lifted off the bottle of Soberano, the ice container, and the two tumblers. 'There you are!' She beamed with pleasure at her success.

Pons hugged her, his expression one of deep love. When he released her, she skipped back into the house. He poured brandy into one glass, pushed the bottle across.

Alvarez helped himself to brandy and ice, said casually: 'The building trade's not doing too well according to what you've been saying.'

'I ain't said nothing.'

'You revised the estimate downwards. No one willingly cuts his own throat.'

'The Germans have all but stopped buying,' Pons muttered.

'And the English?'

'They guard the pesetas. And not many of 'em think of settling in this part of the island.'

'What's up with the Germans?'

'How the hell would I know? Last year they wanted palaces, this year not so much as a barn.'

'So money's really tight?'

'Ain't it always?'

'But there must be some work, even if maybe not so much as there was?'

'Are you a builder? Stick to what you bloody know.'

'Won't the banks help?'

'Ever known 'em to help someone what really needs helping? They only lend to them what's got money and wants more.' Pons finished his drink, poured himself another.

'Things can't be all black.'

'You think working for nothing is good?'

'Seeing you're the best builder around, you've had plenty of work in the past. And the bills for the foreigners will have been generous. So where's all that gone? Maybe you and Pablo have the same story to tell.'

'What Pablo?'

'Comes from my village. Pablo Ramis. Started a carpenter's shop with money borrowed from his aunt, married and had to borrow more to pay his half of the wedding feast because his mother couldn't. Then the foreigners arrived and wanted houses and flats and soon he was employing a dozen men and turning away work. Typically, that's when the trouble started; the time when things finally go right is when they start to go wrong.'

'You're a miserable sod!'

'He was measuring for window frames in a house being built when the Englishman's wife came to the island on her own to see how things were progressing, and according to him – although he's a bit of a liar – she was so eager she had him rolling on the floor before he could close his measurer. From then on, he was like a man who's been hit on the head by a flying cow. They do say he spent twenty million on her, buying jewellery . . .'

Pons thumped the table with his thick fist. 'Are you suggesting I've been spending money on women?'

'I thought . . .'

'If you could think, you wouldn't be in the Cuerpo. I ain't looked at another woman since I married. And what's more, I never will.'

'Would that there were more husbands like you.'

'You don't bloody believe me?'

'Of course I do,' Alvarez answered, sounding insincere.

'I'll tell you where my money went and why I needed that job so bad I dropped the price even if the bastard could have paid twice as much. Some time back . . .'

Alvarez listened and thought how typical of the irony of life that a good deed was not only unrewarded, but it laid the foundations for trouble. For the sake of his parents, Santiago Pons had bailed out his brother, which had left him financially exposed; through valuing three of a kind too highly, exposure had become disaster. Now, although he'd managed to keep afloat, each tomorrow could be the day when he sank . . .

Cristina came out on to the patio. As Pons watched her approach, his love banished the suggestion of taciturn sullenness that his battered, chunky face often held in repose.

'There's nothing wrong, is there?' she asked.

'There's nothing right when the likes of him are around,' Pons replied.

She smiled uneasily. 'You must be old friends to talk like that.'

'I choose my friends.'

She hesitated, then sat. She faced Alvarez. 'Why are you here?'

'Carrying out inquiries following the death of Señor Zavala.'

She said to her husband: 'You did work for him earlier in the year.'

'Because I was a bloody fool.'

Lucía rushed on to the patio, tears tumbling down her cheeks.

'Now what's the matter?' Cristina asked.

'Rosa hit me.'

She cuddled Lucía. 'Why did she hit you?'

'She just did. She's beastly.'

'Let's go inside and sort out the trouble.' She stood, seemed about to speak to Alvarez, but did not, led Lucía inside.

If she were his wife, Alvarez thought, he would be as faithful as Pons claimed to be. She did not resemble Juana-María physically, but he was certain that they had much in common from a character point of view . . . He said to Pons: 'I've a couple more questions.'

'You've more questions than a priest has answers.'

'What cars do you own?'

'What's it to you?' Pons demanded, his previous antagonism returned.

'You've a reason for not answering?'

'I don't like government bastards interfering in my life . . . A Renault and a Citroën van.'

In his office, Alvarez sweated, despite the fan running at full speed. Mallorca was often called the Island of Calm because of its climate. It was a description which also matched the character of the islanders for most of the time. But there were occasions when one of them suffered a sudden rage so violent that he lost all self-control. If Pons had returned to Son Fuyell to appeal once more to be paid the money owed, if Zavala had contemptuously refused, if Pons had seen disaster close even more tightly about himself and the family he loved put to still greater risk, his rage might easily have overwhelmed him. And who could blame him? The law lacked the heart to understand that occasionally legislated wrong was morally right, just as legislated right could be morally wrong. Alvarez sighed.

He looked at the telephone. Salas would be expecting a report. But the superior chief always demanded that every report be comprehensive and until Karen Robertson and Dolly Selby had been questioned, this could not be. Obviously, it was too soon to phone him.

He settled back in the chair and pondered on the vagaries of life so deeply that he awoke only moments before it was time to leave the post and return home.

CHAPTER 13

As Alvarez turned off the road into the drive of Ca'n Jerome, he came bonnet to bonnet with a BMW and had to brake sharply. The woman in the passenger seat gestured angrily at him to back out. He took his time to get out of his Ibiza and walk round to the passenger side of the BMW. Remembering the photograph, he identified the woman inside as Karen Robertson. Not quite as young as he'd thought, but certainly less than half her husband's age; probably blonde by design and not happy chance, though if so, her hairdresser was an expert; beautiful by the standards of the catwalk, which demanded an air of sullen disinterest, no doubt a shapely body, but the sun reflected so fiercely on the half-lowered window that it was impossible to see below the tops of her shoulders . . .

'You'll know me the next time you see me!' She turned to the driver. 'Tell the old fool to get his car out of the way.'

Her companion spoke in good, if stilted, Spanish. 'Would you be kind enough to move so that we can leave here?'

The driver, judging by his features, quietly pitched voice, and somewhat bizarrely coloured, yet obviously expensive, shirt, could well be the man who had driven her to Son Fuyell . . .

'Is he deaf or just plain bloody stupid?' she said.

'Señora, I am not deaf but as to my level of intelligence, I think it is not for me to comment.'

Lockhart said, sotto voce: 'When you're rude, why is it that your listener always speaks your language perfectly?'

'You are Señora Robertson?'

She looked uneasily at Lockhart.

'Sweetie, he's only asking your name, not your age,' Lockhart said.

'But who is he?'

'An interesting point.' He spoke to Alvarez. 'Without becoming too personal, who are you?'

'Inspector Alvarez, Cuerpo General de Policia.'

'A policeman!' Her voice rose. 'What's he want?'

'No doubt he'll soon explain.' Lockhart paused, then added: 'Though on this island, it's safer never to assume anything.'

'Señora,' Alvarez said, 'I am making inquiries following the death of Señor Zavala and should like to ask you some questions.'

'I won't talk about it.'

Lockhart said to Alvarez: 'She has a very sensitive nature and easily becomes disturbed by tragedy.'

'Nevertheless, I regret that it will be necessary for me to speak to her. So if you will back your car, I will drive in and then we can go into the house.'

'I said I won't.' Karen Robertson's voice was shrill. 'It's all too upsetting.'

'I will make every effort not to disturb you any more than is absolutely necessary.'

'I like your style,' Lockhart murmured.

'I don't know anything,' she said wildly.

'Sweetie, I think you have to face the fact that policemen are trained not to recognize negatives.' He looked past her at Alvarez. 'Her overriding concern is for her husband.'

'Of course. But is that relevant?'

'He is a possessive man – who would blame him when he has such riches as she to guard? – and this means that he can respond very deeply on an emotional level. It is disturbing to be questioned by a policeman – even if one has never done anything more reprehensible than suck someone else's Smartie – and if Karen becomes upset, he will become very disturbed. The doctor has repeatedly warned him that because of severe ill-health, he must avoid the slightest emotional storm.'

And if he learned his wife had been enjoying an affair with Zavala, he would suffer an emotional hurricane – or give the appearance of doing so? 'Naturally one does not wish to upset him, but it really is too hot to remain here whilst I talk to the señora.'

'Then let's seek a solution agreeable to both parties, as Zeus said just before he changed into a swan. Would my flat in Port Llueso provide an agreeably neutral sanctum?'

'As you wish.'

'Then if you back on to the road . . .'

'It is always potentially dangerous to do that. So perhaps you will back into the drive to let me enter and turn?'

'Are you a man with a commendable regard for road safety, or one who likes to have the last word?'

'I will leave you to decide that.'

Lockhart laughed as he engaged reverse gear and backed.

Just under half an hour later, Alvarez entered a flat that seemed to him to have been decorated by an anarchist; there was a chaos of colours which assaulted the senses. Only the view through the large picture window of Llueso Bay, quietly, eternally beautiful, offered a sense of harmony.

He sat on a luxuriously comfortable chair covered in a material which didn't just clash with that of the chair next to it, but fought. 'Señor, it will be best if I speak to the señora on her own.'

'I am a very discreet person and good at giving moral support.'

'You think that that will be necessary?'

'I was using the word in a general sense and not in a specific one.'

'For God's sake,' Karen said shrilly, 'can't you ever stop trying to be smart?'

'It's become clear that my services are not only not wanted, they are also not appreciated.' Lockhart stood. 'I shall be in my den and a call will have me running.'

After he'd left, Karen began to fidget with the belt of her dress which, amongst the surrounding clash of colours, looked less smart than it had. She glanced at Alvarez, saw he was regarding her and hurriedly turned away. 'What do you want to know?' she muttered.

'I understand you knew Señor Zavala?'

'Who says I did?'

'Your husband.'

'All he meant was, we'd met him at parties.'

'The friendship was entirely casual?'

'Of course it was.'

'You are quite certain of that?'

'Do I have to tell you ten times before you understand?'

'You did not visit him at his house and when not with your husband?'

'That's a ridiculous question.'

'Why?'

'You can't understand why?'

'I fear I am not conversant with the customs of foreigners.'

'You've got to be bloody ignorant of everything not to realize that if I had seen him at his place, people would have talked.'

'Because you are a married woman?'

'Why else?'

'They would not suppose the relationship to be purely Platonic?'

'The lot who live here? Their favourite occupation after drinking is tearing people's reputations to shreds.'

'Then it is surprising you took such a risk.'

'What are you getting at? Haven't I just said I never visited him on my own?'

'The two maids at Son Fuyell have identified you as a lady who visited Señor Zavala when on her own.'

'They're lying. Their kind always do. It's a way of getting their own back.'

'Why should they want to do that?'

'Because they're so jealous.'

'You don't think that when they see the way in which some foreigners behave, jealousy is their last emotion?'

'I'm not going to be insulted like this.' She got to her

feet and hurried over to the door, pulled it open. 'Theo!' she shouted.

Lockhart ran into the room, almost colliding with her. He came to a stop, studied her. 'You sounded to be at the end of your resistance. But there's not a sign of dishevelled clothing. Did you shout too soon?'

'He's being bloody insulting,' she said furiously.

'It may not be intentional.'

'He's accusing me of visiting Guido on my own, just because the two maids said I did.'

'If that's what they've told him, of course he has to put the possibility to you. All you have to do is laugh at the impossibility.'

'He thinks all foreigners behave badly.'

'Clearly a man of propriety.' He spoke to Alvarez. 'Guido's death has upset her. Not because there was a special relationship between them, but because she takes to heart the solemn warning that any man's death diminishes one. Indeed, a friend has only to suffer and she suffers.'

'Señor Zavala is not suffering.'

'That's a heartless thing to say.'

'Murder is heartless.'

'But are we talking about murder?'

'I am certain you have long since realized that his death may not have been an accident.'

'How easy it is to be certain on other people's behalf.'

'Therefore I need to know the truth of the relationship between the señora and Señor Zavala because it may be significant.'

'I've told you, there wasn't any,' she said wildly.

Alvarez said to Lockhart: 'I understand you frequently take the señora for a drive?'

'Occasionally I have that pleasure.' Lockhart finally sat.

'And at times you have taken her to Son Fuyell?'

'What makes you think that?'

'The evidence of those who saw you.'

'Eye-witness evidence is notoriously inaccurate. Why would I do such a thing?'

89

'Perhaps for the pleasure of knowing you were helping her to betray her marriage.'

'How exquisitely perverse!'

'Tell him that's horrible!' she shouted. 'Tell him you've never taken me there.'

'My angel, we have a problem. Policemen have a nasty habit of becoming annoyed if they believe one's lying to them and they start chuntering about perverting the course of justice – as if justice weren't totally perverted from the beginning. I have to admit that the thought of a Spanish jail positively makes me shiver.'

'God, you're a coward!'

'I would prefer to say that I was born with a reluctance to sacrifice myself, however noble the cause . . . Inspector, you are a man of sharp acumen. Therefore, you will appreciate that black is black only when there is no light. I have driven Karen up to Son Fuyell and left her there, but not for the reason that your imagination no doubt suggests. She is a young lady of great vitality who fell in love with and married a man of considerable presence, but who, being of more years, lacks her energy. Sadly, however much one loves and is loved, in such circumstances there can be moments when one feels a need. She confided in me that when talking to Guido at a party, she mentioned her liking of traditional jazz and how Jerome so hates it that she never listens to it at home. Guido told her that he had an extensive collection of early jazz by the masters, rerecorded and digitally cleaned – whatever that means – sounds slightly dubious – and if ever she wished to listen to some of it, he would be delighted for her to do so. Being by nature chaste, she asked me if I would accompany her, a chaperone beyond the possibility of doubt. My reply was unequivocal. Regretfully, I find all jazz so discordant as to be disturbing. My soul craves quiet consent. To have to listen to it for any length of time would be a penance I wasn't prepared to suffer, not even for her sake. But why should she not go on her own? Honi soit qui mal y pense. Those who knew her would never harbour the slightest doubt that she would observe all the proprieties. Were St Ursula and her eleven thousand virgins doubted? She accepted that that was true. And when I used to drive her home, I never had the slightest doubt that my advice had been faultless. So relaxed and cheerful was she, she had me wondering if my dislike of jazz was mistaken. So there is the truth. What do you say?'

'It is quite a story.'

'If I knew you better, I could judge whether that was said with a naive or a forked tongue.'

Alvarez turned to Karen: 'Señora, you visited Son Fuyell several times?'

'And if I did?'

'Were you always on your own?'

'He's just told you why.'

'Where did Señor Zavala keep his large collection of jazz records – or was it on tape or discs?'

She looked at Lockhart; he examined his fingernails. 'I . . . I can't remember.'

'You have forgotten so quickly?'

'You're confusing me.'

'I am sorry; that is certainly not my intention. But when I searched the house, I found no such collection.'

'I can't help that.'

'Did you always tell your husband when you were going to see Señor Zavala?'

'How could I when I didn't know I was? I'd drive off with Theo and mention how bored I was and he'd suggest taking me to Son Fuyell so that I could hear the music.'

'Why were you bored?'

'This isn't Monte Carlo, for God's sake.'

'After you'd visited Son Fuyell, did you always tell your husband where you'd been?'

'Of course I did.'

'And he never raised any objections to these visits?'

'Why should he?'

'There are husbands who would be disturbed.'

'We trust each other.'

'He didn't ask what happened at Son Fuyell?'

'Nothing happened.'

'Did you sometimes break off from listening to the music to go down to the pool and have a swim?'

She hesitated. 'I might have done when it was very hot.'

'So you always carried a costume with you?'

'Yes.'

'But there was at least one time when you didn't bother to wear it, wasn't there?'

'No. What are you suggesting now?'

'That you sunbathed, and almost certainly swam, in the nude.'

'Of course I didn't.'

'The gardener claims to have seen you by the pool without a costume on.'

'He's a dirty old man, like Emilio who can't look at me without mentally undressing me.'

'The gardener is lying?'

'Yes.'

'I have to tell you that it will be entirely in your own interests to confirm that that is so since then I will have no reason to question you further and you will be saved any unfortunate embarrassment. Will you be prepared to prove you have been speaking the truth?'

'Sweetie, don't be rash . . .' Lockhart began.

'Of course I will,' she snapped.

'Then I shall arrange a time that is convenient to both you and the doctor.'

'Doctor? What's he to do with it?'

'Lorenzo Frau told me that you had what he described as a birthmark on your buttocks. When a doctor tells me you carry no such mark, I will know Lorenzo is a liar.'

Her expression tightened. She cleared her throat. 'I . . .'

'Yes, señora?'

'I've just remembered. There was one time when I'd forgotten to take my costume, but it was so hot that I thought just for once it would be all right to swim with nothing on. How was I to know that the beastly man was a Peeping Tom?'

'So it is you who are the liar, not Lorenzo?'

'I forgot. I tell you, I forgot.'

'As you seem to have forgotten that on this occasion Señor Zavala was with you and he also was without clothes.'

'Theo, you've got to help me,' she cried desperately.

'Sweetie, mendacem memorem esse oportet or, to paraphrase freely, when a lie threatens to catch up with you, either shake it by the hand or run like hell.'

'You bastard!'

'I hope so. My mother always swore her husband fathered me, but through choice I've never believed her.'

She began to cry.

'Señora,' Alvarez said, concealing his scorn, 'I am not concerned with the life you choose to lead. But I must know something. Has your husband ever accused you of having an affair with Señor Zavala?'

She shook her head.

'Even if he has never directly accused you, might he have suspected?'

'No.'

'How can you be so certain?'

'He's so jealous, he'd have created hell . . . You won't tell him, will you? I swear it didn't mean anything. It's just . . . Please understand. Jerome's so dull and always moaning he's ill and Guido was so alive and different . . . Please, don't tell Jerome.'

'Señora, if there is no cause to do so, I will not.'

'Oh, God, why did we stay by the pool instead of going up to the house?'

A question, Alvarez thought, which perfectly summed up her character. He stood, said a polite goodbye, left. He had stepped out of the flat into the small square when Lockhart appeared in the doorway. 'You should display a warning, Inspector. Do not take me at face value.'

Even by the time he reached his car, Alvarez still couldn't be certain whether that had been an insult or a compliment.

CHAPTER 14

Alvarez awoke, but did not open his eyes. When sleep had departed, but reality not fully intervened, a man could float on a cloud above the world and all its troubles . . . A shout from below brought him crashing down to earth.

'Enrique, are you ever going to get up?'

Women seemed constitutionally incapable of relaxing and so, because of their selfish natures, made certain men never had the chance to do so.

'It's after five o'clock.'

Time should not be worshipped; a slave, not a master.

'If you don't come down right away, there'll be no hot chocolate because I have to go out.'

He climbed off the bed, put on shirt and trousers, went along to the bathroom to wash his face in cold water.

Dolores was standing by the kitchen table, reading a book. 'If you spend any more time in your bed, you'll grow roots,' she said, without looking up.

'I had a very stressful morning.'

'Then you shouldn't have drunk so much at lunch. Alcohol is the worst possible thing for stress.'

'That's ridiculous!'

'You are an expert in medical matters; the doctor on television knows nothing?'

'Doctors, especially on the telly, get bees in their bonnets . . .'

'Better than worms in their brains. The chocolate's on the stove. It may have become lumpy because you've taken so long to come down.' She looked up. 'Aren't you supposed to be back at the post by four-thirty?'

'The hours are not fixed exactly.'

'Not by you, that's for certain.' She looked back at the

book. 'There's some coca in the cupboard if you left any yesterday.'

'But that'll be stale . . .'

She jerked her head up. 'So! I am expected to go out every day, no matter how exhausted, to buy fresh coca for my cousin so that when he can find the energy to come downstairs, it is waiting for him?'

'I thought you made it . . .'

'In the heat of the summer, when men find it impossible to do anything but eat, drink, and sleep, I should not only slave all day preparing two full meals, I should also exhaust myself beyond recovery to make you coca because you have too delicate a palate for any that is not fresh?'

He crossed to a cupboard and brought out the triangle of coca on a plate. When in her present mood, it was no good pointing out how illogical and selfish she was being. He put a mug on the table, lifted the saucepan off the stove and filled the mug with hot chocolate. Of course, basically Jaime was at fault. A husband should at the beginning of a marriage make it clear who was boss in the house.

He ate and drank.

'We have not had Pilotes amb safrà for a long time,' she said suddenly. She shut the book with a snap.

He cheered up. 'You're going to cook that?'

'Why should I bother when it would be eaten with careless indifference?'

'Each mouthful will be sweeter than a maiden's kiss because you are the finest cook on the island.'

'Because I am fool enough to spend my life in slavery.' But her tone had changed. What he had said was true. 'I am going shopping. So be certain to lock up.' She picked up her purse and left.

He began to eat the coca. Meatballs could be just an apology for food, yet when Dolores wove her magic over the ground pork, beef, ham, bacon, eggs, onions, garlic, breadcrumbs, lard, lemon juice, parsley, nutmeg, saffron, pepper and salt, they became a Lucullan feast . . . She was at times irrational, illogical, and very unreasonable, but in all fairness one had to make allowances for the fact that she was a woman. And truly a wonderful cook.

Alvarez had never fully understood the expression 'blue-rinse lady' until he faced Dolly Selby.

'It is an impertinence,' she said.

She undoubtedly regarded almost everything as an impertinence, he thought gloomily. Judging by the attempts to camouflage her age, she was probably well past her allotted span and into extra time; her hair was not blue-rinsed, but neither was it naturally coloured and, since she'd left him to stand, he could make out where it was thinning; her nose was beaky, her lips full and moist, but the only passion they suggested was greed; she wore a finca and many good hectares of rich land on her fingers and a manorial house on her over-generous bosom.

A young woman, dressed in a neat, striped maid's frock, came across the lawn of gama grass to where Dolly sat in the shade of an ancient evergreen oak. 'Señora, a telephone,' she said in fractured English.

'What's that?'

'Someone speaks . . .'

'I think there is a telephone call for you, señora,' Alvarez said.

'Thank you, but I am quite capable of understanding . . . Where's the cordless phone, you stupid girl? Why didn't you bring it with you?'

The maid looked confused.

'The cordless phone,' she said loudly and held her clenched fist up to her ear.

The maid hurried into the house.

'The brains of a rabbit,' Dolly said.

Better than the manners of a bitch. 'Señora, I need to ask you . . .'

'Wait.'

He sat on the second chair, an action which clearly annoyed her. The maid returned, handed Dolly a cordless phone, left. Dolly languidly and at length discussed the incompetence of the local workmen and the stupidity of all staff.

She finally said goodbye, switched off the phone, put it down on the table to her right.

'Señora, I should like to ask you about the party you gave a week ago, yesterday.'

'It is an impertinence to concern yourself in my affairs.'

'Señor Zavala drowned in his swimming pool . . .'

'Do you wish to suggest I am in any way concerned with that fact?'

'Of course not.'

'Then there is nothing more to be said.'

'I wish to ask you questions concerning Señor Zavala.'

'Why?'

'I understand you were a friend of his.'

'Even in these dreadful socialist times when we are not supposed to say what we think, we are still left at liberty to choose our friends. He was an acquaintance.'

'You did not like him?'

'He was not a gentleman. Of course, that's not surprising since he was an Argentinian.'

'Actually, señora, he was a Bolivian.'

'There's no difference.'

'There is to a Bolivian or an Argentinian.'

'You seem intent on being insolent.'

'Señora, would you like to be thought Italian?'

'No one could seriously make such a suggestion.'

'That is true.'

She stared angrily at him, but his battered face held such a woebegone expression that she decided it was absurd to believe he had the intelligence to have been inferring anything.

'Señora, is it correct that during the course of your party, you introduced Señor Zavala to Señor and Señora Bailey?'

'Quite possibly.'

'You cannot be certain?'

'I see no reason to be.'

'It could be important.'

She sighed heavily and her bosom surged. 'Yes, I introduced them.'

'Why did you do that?'

'What an extraordinary question! Do you people have no idea of social manners?'

'Indeed, señora, but in many cases they are different from yours.'

'Unfortunately! It is the duty of a hostess to make certain that all her guests meet.'

'And the Baileys did not know Señor Zavala before you introduced them?'

'Do try to use a little common sense. Would I have needed to introduce them if they knew each other?'

'Do you think Señor Zavala had any idea who they were before you introduced them?'

'Really, this is like trying to explain something to a five-year-old. If they had never met, how could Guido know who they were?'

'It is possible to know who someone is before one meets that person.'

'Really?'

'Did the Baileys later speak to you about Señor Zavala?'

'What do you mean?'

'Did they ask you where he lived, how long he'd been on the island – that sort of thing?'

'You can't be expected to realize this, but it is bad manners to ask personal questions and the Baileys do have manners. Only . . .'

'Yes, señora?'

'It has to be admitted that they did behave rather strangely.'

'You are now saying that they did ask many questions about Señor Zavala?'

'You seem incapable of understanding anything. I was not referring to that, but to the fact that very soon after I'd introduced them to Guido, they left, before the party was half over and without thanking me for inviting them. Hardly the behaviour expected if they really are the right kind of people, as they try to make out.'

'Perhaps one of them suddenly felt ill?'

'Hardly an adequate excuse.'

'Did they later explain to you why they had left so suddenly?'

'They did not.'

'Did Señor Zavala later make any comment about them to you?'

'No. Though he had the manners to thank me for having invited him. A bit too flowery with his thanks, of course, but one can't expect too much when one invites him into one's circle.'

He stood, said goodbye, and was amused when her only response was a curt nod of the head.

As Alvarez drove up the main road from the port to the village, he wondered whether the explanation for the Baileys' behaviour was, in fact, that one of them had become ill? But then wouldn't the other have mentioned the fact, however briefly? Had it been their meeting with Zavala which had so disturbed them? Yet how could a brief meeting between strangers have such consequences?

There was something here that might be important, but he was damned if he could begin to work out what it might be.

The Laboratory of Forensic Sciences phoned at twenty past seven.

'We've been working in conjunction with the Institute and can now say that the fingerprints on the glass and bottle are all Zavala's; likewise, the hairs are from his head. While some hairs have been broken off, many have been pulled out by their roots. The blood on the patio chair was his.'

'Would it require much force to have pulled the hairs out?'

'Singly, no; all together, a reasonable amount.'

'Is there any way of judging which happened?'

'No.'

'Suppose he'd fallen into the pool and someone was holding his head under with a scoop until he drowned, would you expect a mixture of broken hairs and hairs torn out by the roots?'

'If he was fully conscious and struggling, almost certainly; if unconscious, or even badly dazed, it would be a question of how much force had to be used to keep his head under.'

'If he was conscious and someone was using the scoop not to force his head under, but to keep it raised, or he was unconscious and that someone was trying to keep his nose above the water, but eventually failed, one would expect the would-be rescuer to try to have called for help.'

'Logical.'

'Can you suggest any other way those hairs could have reached the skimming net, apart from the obvious one that they fell out naturally?'

'With their roots? And nine times out of ten, when a person has finished scooping the surface of a pool, he shakes out the net.'

'Would that dislodge them all?'

'I've no idea. Find out by testing with your own hairs. But remember, you'll need to carry out a large number of tests in order to gain a statistical probability. Are you prepared to go bald in the pursuit of justice?'

People who worked in the laboratory had almost as poor a sense of humour as those in the Institute. Not conscious of what he was doing, Alvarez fingered the hairs on the crown of his head to convince himself that he was not, as Juan had so rudely suggested a few days before, becoming bald.

CHAPTER 15

'That is all you've been able to learn?' Salas asked sharply over the phone.

'Unfortunately, señor, much of the evidence is rather ambiguous . . .'

'Do you know the definition of ambiguity? A sophist's excuse.'

Alvarez doggedly continued. 'However, it does seem more likely that Zavala was murdered than drowned accidentally. There is the blow to his throat, the hairs in the skimming net . . .'

'There is no need to repeat yourself yet again.'

'This means someone had the motive to murder him. I have identified one person with a motive – Santiago Pons, whose business is under severe financial threat because Zavala refused to pay him what was due; one person who may well have a motive – Señor Robertson, whose wife was having an affair with Zavala and she has admitted that her husband is very jealous and given to anger; and one person who does not appear to have a motive, yet who is identified with Zavala through the evidence and therefore probably does have one even if this has not yet been established . . .'

'To be illogical is to be lazy. You tell me, if there has been murder, there was motive. I will not disagree with that, although it is fact that there are occasionally motiveless murders. You name one man with a certain motive, another with a probable one which necessitates Señor Robertson being aware of his wife's infidelity . . . It really is quite extraordinary how so many cases with which you are connected become coated with immorality.'

'They concern foreigners.'

'I wish I could be convinced that that is the reason.'

'I only uncover what is already there . . .'

'Kindly stick to matters which are pertinent.'

'Yes, señor. It is true that until we can prove Señor Robertson knew of his wife's affair, we cannot say for certain he had a motive for the murder, but he must have accepted the probability that she would betray him . . .'

'Why do you say that?'

'There is such a difference in their ages.'

'You cannot accept that that is of no consequence when couples – even foreign couples – trust each other?'

'Human nature being what it is . . .'

'I am happy to believe human nature to be on a far higher plane than you so clearly place it. A pure mind sees light where the impure mind sees shadow. You should try to remember that.'

'Yes, señor. Only isn't it our job to uncover the shadows beneath the light?'

'Finish your report without all these ridiculous diversions.'

'If suspicious because of jealousy, it's very possible he wondered about his wife's frequent car trips with Señor Lockhart . . .'

'I suppose you are now going to suggest that she's also been having an affair with him?'

'Most unlikely.'

'Why, when you are so ready to assume an affair with Zavala?'

'Señor Lockhart is . . . She will not have attracted him, if you understand?'

'I do not.'

'From observing him, I would judge him to be one of them.'

'One of whom?'

'Not sexually interested in women.'

'My God, man, your mind's a sewer! Have you ever been examined by a psychiatrist?'

'No, señor.'

'I suggest you do so as soon as possible before it becomes

impossible to effect any improvement. Now, kindly make a proper report.'

'As I've mentioned, on the face of things, Señor Bailey has no motive. But the car that was seen leaving Son Fuyell within a few hours of the estimated time of death has been identified as a new model Astra shooting brake, dark-coloured, and he owns one. Admittedly, we cannot unreservedly accept that identification, not only because it was dark – although there was a full, or nearly full, moon – but because of the circumstances.'

'What circumstances?'

'Ferriol and Inés had parked in the clump of trees near the entrance to the estate and then put a blanket down on the ground just outside the trees and . . . Well, at such times, obviously one is not very concerned about anything else and so not keenly or accurately observant.'

'You are talking in riddles. Kindly explain in simple terms why Ferriol's description of the car should be treated with such caution.'

'The two of them were screwing . . .'

'Enough! I will not have you fuelling your perverted pleasure with gutter language.'

'Would you prefer me to say, fornicating?'

'If you find it absolutely necessary to refer to the subject in the first place.'

'I'm sure it has to be held in mind.'

'Not in my mind.'

'When a couple are fornicating, their attention is focused entirely on themselves; this certainly holds good before and during and then for quite some time after they . . .'

'Kindly remember I do not share your delight in revelling in such details.'

'What it adds up to is this: I suggest one has to regard the identification of the car as probably good, but just possibly mistaken. Of the three men, Señor Bailey has a new model Astra shooting brake, green-coloured. A fact which gains significance when there is a connection between him and Señor Zavala.'

'What is the connection?'

'I don't know.'

'How very typical!'

'There is good reason for believing that up until a cocktail party at midday on the Tuesday, the two men had never met. At the party they were introduced and for probably no more than ten minutes they spoke together. Then Señor Bailey and his wife left, so abruptly that they did not thank their hostess; I understand that this is a custom the English always observe, so their failure to do so surely must have significance. But is it feasible that after meeting someone for the first time, he can say something so immediately dramatic, traumatic, distressing . . .'

'This is not a theatrical conversation.'

'It may seem impossible that so brief a conversation with a stranger could seed a murder, but the one did follow the other. I don't believe that can have been pure coincidence. I have the feeling that this meeting and its aftermath are the key to events, even if at the moment such a proposition appears to fly in the face of logic.'

'A flight you are seldom reluctant to make.'

'In my opinion, we should look into the past lives of the two men as far as that proves possible.'

'Because in the past lies the motive for Zavala's murder? Have you forgotten that there is as yet no certainty he was murdered?'

'Yet if we find Señor Bailey had a strong motive, then we can be reasonably certain he was.'

'You assume that if there was a strong motive, there was murder; Bailey appears to have no motive, so you presume murder in order to hold he must, in fact, have had one.'

'It may seem a little strange . . .'

'It does.'

'But it surely has to be worth discovering if there was some previous connection between the two men? So I think I should . . .'

'If you are about to suggest a trip to England, don't bother. You are not going to use this case as an excuse to indulge in your passion for holidays abroad at the department's expense.'

'But I am certain . . .'

'And I am even more certain that you will remain on this island, pursuing your duties in so far as you ever find this possible. A request will be forwarded to England to ask if they can supply any background history which might prove significant.' Salas cut the connection.

Alvarez thought how odd it was that rank always bred suspicion. True, he had been about to suggest he should go to England, but he had been motivated by duty, not an irresponsible desire to holiday.

He pulled open the bottom right-hand drawer of the desk and brought out a bottle of brandy and a glass. Little so upset a man as to have his motives misunderstood.

CHAPTER 16

The detective inspector had unexpectedly been called out of the station and Detective Constable Perry seized the opportunity to slip into the DI's office to read his confidential report. 'This officer,' it concluded, 'must learn to constrain his imagination since at times it lifts his judgement into the realms of soothsaying.' Sarcastic bastard! he thought, as he returned to the CID general room and sat at his desk. Had the DI never listened over-trustingly to an informer?

He looked up as Yates entered and crossed to the corner desk. Rank always used whatever clout was going. That corner of the room was warmer in the winter and cooler in the summer – if there was one.

'Lewis, come over here, will you?' Yates called out.

Perry pushed back his chair and crossed the room. 'Something moving, Sarge?'

'I've had the old man moaning again about misspellings in the reports. He wants the word passed around to all you bright ignorami that someone's invented a thing called a dictionary. More importantly, there's a request from Spain, through Interpol; from Majorca, to be exact.' Yates was exact by nature. Nearing the end of his service, he had his quiet, peaceful retirement carefully planned, much to his wife's concern, who had hoped he would find a job as a security guard and not be around the house all day, every day.

Perry spoke nostalgically. 'I had a couple of weeks in Majorca a year or two back; a place called Portals Nous. They're right. It is all sun, sea, sand, sangria and sex.'

'I'm too old for the details . . . They want any information we can give 'em concerning Harry Charles Bailey, now living on the island, last address here, Ekstone House, West Angleton.'

'That's a ritzy area. Like as not, he's a tax-dodger.'

'Good luck to him if he is. Aged forty-one, married to Fenella Pamela, maiden name Lyon.'

'I knew a Fenella.'

'With any luck, she'll have overcome the experience. Try to find something to make 'em feel we've done our best.'

'Have we been told what this is in aid of?'

'Bailey's a possible suspect in a possible murder.'

'Sounds all very uncertain.'

'It's Spain.'

Perry returned to his desk, picked up a pen and clipped it in his inside pocket, left the room. He hadn't thought about Fenella for a long time. She'd been a classy blonde – or had she been a brunette? – her only fault, slightly protruding teeth which tended to get in the way – unless he was mixing her up with Helen? Anyway, whichever, the only thing she hadn't liked had been the sangria.

It was late afternoon when Perry met Yates in the corridor which led from the charge room to the front room. 'Sarge.'

Yates came to a stop. Always large, he was now putting on considerable weight despite his wife's attempts to persuade him to curb his appetite.

'I've a lead on Bailey.'

'Let's hear it.'

'He's an ex-con.'

'Is he, now? What did he go down for?'

'Causing death by dangerous driving and driving under the influence.'

'How long did he earn?'

'A fiver.'

'Sounds as if it was a nasty case.'

'I reckon it must have been. The OiC was a detective superintendent.'

'For a traffic case?'

'I'll say it's got to have been more than appeared in court.'

'Knowing you, I suppose you'll suggest Bailey was in drag and propositioned the arresting officer.'

'Bloody funny.'

'Make the report, check for spelling, let me have it to pass on to the old man who'll ship it off to Majorca.' Yates took a pace forward.

'Sarge, don't you think that first I ought to find out if there were any special circumstances which caused a DS to be in charge?'

'Not enough work of our own so we can afford to waste time on other people's?'

'Then I don't check any deeper?'

Yates hesitated. He had never made detective inspector because he lacked the ambition necessary to accept the responsibility; he had made detective sergeant because he was stolidly efficient and knew how to defend his back. If there were unusual circumstances to this case and these might prove helpful to an ongoing investigation, Spain needed to be informed; if it ever became known that he was responsible for their being withheld, he'd be in the mud. 'Dig around, but don't make a big meal out of it.'

Perry reread his notes. Bailey, in a Jaguar, had struck a young girl and thrown her to the side of the road on the outskirts of Halfchurch. He'd driven on, to return a few minutes later, arriving after the ambulance and the police. He had been breathalysed and as the reading had been positive, had undergone a blood test. That confirmed he had been just above the limit and he had been arrested and his car impounded for examination. The child had died soon after the accident. Bailey had been tried in Halfchurch, found guilty, and sentenced to five years in jail. He had served just under half the sentence.

Perry tapped on the desk with his fingers. On the face of things, a tragic but straightforward traffic accident either caused by drink or one which would probably have been avoided if the driver had not been drinking. In normal circumstances, the investigating officer would have been of a lower rank than detective superintendent.

He dialled HQ, A Division, spoke to a woman who passed

him on to a man who passed him on to a second man who said that no, he couldn't help with any of the details of the case, it would be a job to search through the records, the odds had to be there was nothing more to be learned . . . Perry was familiar with the procedure since he used it himself many times. 'My DI's curious.' Rank always counted. 'There's something pretty odd about the case.'

'Really!'

'Detective Superintendent Turpin was OiC.'

'Was he?'

'Why would someone of his rank handle a straightforward traffic incident, even if there was a fatality?'

'I've no idea.'

'I suppose he'd be able to answer that?'

'Could be.'

'I'll try and have a word with him, then.'

'You do that.'

Perry said goodbye, replaced the receiver, looked across at the DC who sat two desks away. 'Pat, didn't Superintendent Turpin at County HQ retire last year?'

'Yeah. It's Varley now.'

He spoke to a sergeant at county who gave him Turpin's home address and telephone number and then gratuitously added the comment that according to some, retirement had so softened him he could almost be pleasant.

He phoned the number and spoke to a woman who said she'd have a word with her husband. As he waited, he tried to identify of whom her voice reminded him and came to the conclusion it was the maths teacher at his primary school.

'He could find time tomorrow morning,' she said.

'That's great.'

'Will ten-thirty be all right?'

'I'll be there on the dot.'

He thanked her, rang off. The maths teacher had tried to inculcate in him a love of the subject. She must have become a very frustrated woman.

Turpin lived in a small country cottage that was surrounded

by fields and backed by woods; as Perry climbed out of the CID Escort, he heard the harsh call of a cock pheasant, declaring its readiness for love or determination to defend its territory – he wasn't certain which. Even the leaden sky, the drizzle, and the cold wind couldn't lessen his sense of pleasure. Despite being city born, it was his ambition to live in the country.

A gravel path led to a wooden gate and beyond was a well-tended garden and a brick path that took him to the front door. The pheasant called again as he rang the bell, set in the wooden frame. The door was opened by a woman who dressed for comfort rather than style. 'Come on in. Dreadful day, isn't it? More like October than July.'

In appearance, she wasn't at all like the maths teacher, who had been angular and possessor of an ever-runny nose. She showed him into a small sitting room which had a beamed ceiling and a large, wide inglenook fireplace. 'George won't be a moment . . .' She stopped as her husband entered.

'Good morning, sir,' Perry said. Rank ceased on retirement, but it always massaged egos to continue to observe it. 'Kind of you to take the time to see me.'

'No bother. There's nothing to do on a day like this.'

'The chairs,' she said.

'They're not forgotten.'

'Just put to the back of the mind?'

'They'll get done. Now, how about some coffee?'

'That's all in hand.' She left the room, closing the door behind her.

'Grab a chair,' Turpin said. 'D'you smoke?'

'No, thank you.'

'According to the media, every time I light a cigarette, I'm shaking hands with the undertaker. Yet my father and uncle smoked like chimneys and both died of old age.' He lit a cigarette. 'I gather you want to discuss a case I was connected with. Which one?'

Perry answered the question.

'Bailey?' Turpin said reflectively. 'A thoroughly decent, likeable chap. The fact his wife divorced him must have made his stay in stir that much tougher.' He tapped the ash off his cigarette into an ashtray that was in front of a vase of roses. 'I remember the case more clearly than most because it was a one-off. Not that at the beginning it looked in any way unusual . . . What's your particular angle?'

'To find out if there's anything about Bailey which would help the Spanish police in their inquiries into a possible murder case.'

'I'll tell you what I can and you judge . . . I wasn't called in initially because the facts of the case seemed perfectly straightforward. Bailey was driving home one wet night and passing through Halfchurch when he hit an eleven-year-old girl. He didn't stop. Some time later – as much as twenty minutes, I seem to recall – he returned to the scene and was interviewed by the crew of a patrol car. He was breathalysed and as he was just over the limit, was taken to the station for a blood sample. He was arrested for being under the influence. News came through that the girl had died from her injuries and he was charged with the much more serious offence.

'He made a voluntary statement. He claimed he had drunk some wine with his meal and had considered himself perfectly capable of driving, but accepted that he'd been over the legal limit. While going along the road in the outskirts of Halfchurch . . .'

His wife entered, carrying a tray which she put down on the occasional table that was between the two men. 'Help yourselves; and I've put out some digestive biscuits.'

Turpin said: 'There are only two cups – aren't you having some?'

'I must see if Matilda wants any shopping done today.'

'Is her leg no better?'

'To listen to her, it's worse, but I suspect she's milking sympathy as hard as she can.'

'Then stop being a milch cow.'

'Come on, the poor old girl's over eighty. When we reach that age, we'll want all the sympathy we can grab.' She turned to Perry. 'Can I offer you anything more?'

'No, thank you, Mrs Turpin.'

'Then I'll be off.'

'Make certain you're well wrapped up,' her husband said.

'Don't worry, I will.' She left.

As Turpin spooned sugar into a cup, a gust of wind drove rain, which had overtaken the drizzle, against the single window with a harsh, drumming sound. 'And they tell us it's summer! I'll bet half my pension that in Majorca the sun's shining and the sea's like a warm bath. Add in good, cheap wine and fried squid and what more could a man want?'

Perry did not answer that it depended how old the man was. One evening, when it was dark, Fenella – or had she been Helen? – had dared him to join her swimming naked . . .

Turpin lit another cigarette. 'I was telling you about Bailey's statement. He was driving with all due care and attention – ever met a motorist who wasn't? – when a car tailgated him with flashing headlights. He refused to be hurried so the Jaguar pulled out and overtook and then cut back very tightly across Bailey's bonnet in a motorist's two-finger. The road was wet, the overtaking car suddenly skidded and the next thing he knew was that something was thrown up into the air by the Jaguar to come back to hit his near-side wing; it was only then that he identified the something as a body. He didn't stop. He returned later.'

'Did he say why he didn't stop?'

'He claimed he was so shocked by events that he hadn't been able to pull himself together right away . . . The time gap seemed a bit long for that sort of reaction, not that you can ever be certain how people are going to react, and this did briefly have me wondering if he'd had a woman or, this being the age it is, maybe a man, in the car and had been trying desperately to keep that information to himself. But there was never anything to say one way or the other.'

'Could he have been tight enough to think at first he'd get away with it, but then decided that was too risky?'

'That was an obvious possibility, but it didn't seem to fit his character . . .' Turpin became silent. He picked up his cup and drained it.

'It sounds a straightforward traffic incident – one driver under the influence, the other who thinks he's a Schumacher, a kid who's in the wrong place at the wrong time – why were you called in instead of leaving the case with the divisional DI?'

'The interesting bit is to come.' Turpin lit yet another cigarette. 'Because Bailey had been so incensed by the stupidity and recklessness of the driver of the Jaguar, he'd made a mental note of the registration number and despite the shock – or even perhaps because of it – he was able to quote this in his statement. When the number was fed into the computer, up came the Bolivian embassy in London as registered owners.'

Perry whistled.

'Just so! Trouble, in underlined capitals! I'm called in to keep things cool, the bureaucrats wet their knickers more than usual, every detail of the case is viewed from twenty different angles before the embassy is contacted.

'They denied their Jaguar had been involved in any accident that night, or any other night. Questions were put with as much tact as if we'd been talking to a load of nuns in a rape case. Had the car been on the road that night? No. Who normally drove it? The chauffeur assigned to it. His name? The embassy was not at liberty to disclose the names of any who worked for it. Where was the harm in naming him if he had not been involved in the incident? No comment. Could the car be examined to confirm it had not been in an accident and that the eyewitness evidence was false? Certainly not. Why not? No comment.

'Since a successful defence obviously depended on Bailey's version of events being accepted, his lawyers decided to flush out the chauffeur so that he could be questioned. The moment they set the wheels in motion, the embassy claimed the man was part of the ambassadorial suite and therefore enjoyed diplomatic immunity. Since chauffeurs don't normally enjoy that degree of status, the defence challenged the assertion. A member of the embassy confirmed the claim and a Foreign Office certificate to that effect was issued; this meant that no court could traverse the certificate to determine whether the chauffeur really was entitled to immunity.

'The defence team were high-powered and at the trial they pulled out all the stops. Bailey had been over the alcohol limit, but only just; he had been in full control of himself. He had not stopped immediately, because he had been so shocked it had taken him time to recover – the fact that he had returned proved this. The victim had been struck first by the Jaguar and even if cold sober, he would have had absolutely no chance of avoiding hitting her. Prosecution witnesses had agreed that in view of the very serious injuries the victim had suffered, they would have expected to find considerably greater damage to his car – their claim that this did not prove his contention that when the victim struck his car this was a secondary blow, was clearly unsustainable. He had named the other car as a Jaguar when giving the number to the police and had said it was white in colour. That number did belong to a white Jaguar, so it would be a coincidence too far to believe he had pulled it out of the air to add a suggestion of verisimilitude. The fact that the Jaguar belonged to a foreign embassy which refused to allow the car to be examined strongly suggested . . . The judge jumped very quickly on that and expressed his great surprise that so eminent a silk should try to introduce evidence through the back door which he knew could not be introduced through the front door . . .

'All in all, the defence put up a good fight and the verdict might well have gone in Bailey's favour – as far as the more serious charge was concerned, of course – if he had only presented himself better in the witness box. But he seemed . . . The best I can say is, he didn't project the emotional urgency which a man can be expected to do when he's struggling to make people understand he's telling the truth; he seemed almost resigned to being disbelieved.'

'Yet you said earlier that most of the time you reckoned he was telling the truth?'

'That's right.'

'Then why should he have been resigned?'

'Perhaps because he wanted to be.'

'I'm afraid I don't get that.'

'You can still meet someone who lives by standards. He'd

have been called a gentleman in the days when that was a mark of respect rather than sarcasm. I reckon something had happened which caused him to feel guilty, guilt deserved punishment, therefore he must suffer punishment. Perhaps confirmation that he'd had a woman in the car who shouldn't have been there? . . . And now he's suspected of murder?'

'The Spanish police don't go that far, but it's clear they think him a possible suspect in a possible murder. There is one last thing, sir.'

'Which is?'

'Can you give me the names of the chauffeur and whoever it was who granted him diplomatic immunity?'

'I seem to remember defence counsel managed to flush out both, but what they were, I haven't the slightest idea.'

'They're probably on record. So do you think you could be very kind and check them out?'

'You're asking me to spend my retirement ploughing through ancient files?'

'It would be a little more information to feed through to Majorca. These days, the buzz word is PR and it would be a good move to make the blokes over there realize how much trouble we've taken on their behalf.'

'You think they'll give a damn? Public relations? An excuse for incompetence!'

CHAPTER 17

Alvarez mopped his forehead, cheeks and neck with a handker-chief. It was not a hot summer; it was a summer straight from the fires of hell; it left a man struggling to find the energy to keep his eyes open . . .

One of the two female civilians at the post walked into his office. Spain had enthusiastically embraced the theory of sexual equality in the workforce; before some sections of the workforce responded, the female intake would need to be more feminine. 'Fax,' she said, her voice grainy, as if she had been working the fields for hours without a drink. 'It's your job to collect 'em.'

'I didn't know there was one to collect.'

'Been trying to get hold of you for long enough. Spend your time asleep, I suppose.' She slapped the fax down on the desk, left. He wondered how much longer her linen slacks would withstand the strain they were under.

He read the fax, whistled, looked up at a gecko on the ceiling. 'What is the superior chief going to say to this?' The gecko did not answer, but looked as if it could guess.

Zavala had awarded Rojas Algaro diplomatic immunity, which meant the defence had been unable to prove Bailey's claim that the Jaguar had hit the girl first, sending her up into the air to brush his car. To know that a man had prevented one from proving one's innocence, had condemned one to a prison sentence, was cause for wild thoughts and dreams of revenge throughout the incarceration; unexpectedly to meet a man at a cocktail party and learn from his boasting that he was not just a Zavala, but *the* Zavala, was to discover that the means for revenge were to hand . . .

Was this motive stronger than those of Robertson and

Pons? Only they could accurately judge how strongly their motives drove them. But what was certain was that of the three, only Bailey owned an Astra shooting brake . . .

What should his next move be? Did he act and then inform Salas; did he first inform Salas of his intended action? It was a tricky decision. He decided to make it over a cup of coffee and a brandy.

He was within a hundred metres of the Club Llueso, trying to edge his way through a drifting stream of tourists who had been brought to the village by bus, when a voice behind him said: 'Mr Holmes, I presume.'

He came to a stop and turned to face Lockhart. 'No, señor, Inspector Alvarez of the Cuerpo General de Policia.'

'Now is that a naively innocent reply, or one carefully constructed to make me look foolish? . . . You intrigue me, Inspector, though for your peace of mind I hasten to add, only in an intellectual sense. You possess that gift, invaluable to anyone who has reason to hide the course of his thoughts, of being able to look vacuous even when most cerebrally active.'

'How can that be certain if my expression is so vacant?'

'The more I see of you, the more I appreciate you. Come and have a coffee.'

'I don't think I have the time.'

'On this island, still an outpost of gracious living, time has no meaning.'

'My superior chief would not agree.'

'Superiors never agree with anything, which is why they are so superior. Please don't deprive me of your company.'

Alvarez followed Lockhart up the steps to the higher part of the square and across to where tables and chairs were set out in front of one of the cafés. As they sat in the shade of a sun umbrella, a waiter hurried across, suggesting Lockhart was a regular customer who was liberal with his tips.

'What would you like?' Lockhart asked.

'Coffee cortado, please.'

'And a coñac to go with it, of course. You have the measure of a man who makes a point of observing custom.' He gave the order, produced a silver cigarette case. 'Do you smoke?'

'Regrettably, yes.'

'Regret your virtues, not your vices; throughout history, virtue has caused far greater disasters than vice ever has.' He opened the case and Alvarez took a cigarette, then flicked a lighter for both of them. He drew on his cigarette, said: 'Pander to my enjoyment of the inessential and tell me if the case of the drowned diplomat is solved?'

'Not yet.'

'Was it murder?'

'Even that isn't certain.'

'Excellent! Mysteries need time to mature.'

'Señor . . .'

'The name is Theodore. My parents had an unfortunate sense of humour.'

'Do you think Señor Robertson suspected his wife was having an affair with Señor Zavala?'

'You are asking me to betray friendship?'

'Did you not betray it each time you drove the señora to Son Fuyell?'

'There is acid behind the soft soap? No, inspector of morals, I did not. My friendship is with Karen, whom I love dearly because she is amusing and supremely selfish. By contrast, Jerome is the kind of man who demands to be betrayed when he is not ignored. A little man from the outer suburbs of some ghastly town, he made a lot of money and lacks the wit to spend it elegantly. He'll repeat the latest stock market figures with unseemly relish, but try to talk about the genius of Velázquez and he'll tell you he has no interest in Spanish football.'

'He must have wondered why the señora and you so often went for a drive.'

'If so, it would only to have been to question her taste of companion.'

The waiter returned and put cups, milk, sugar, and two glasses, down on the table, spiked the bill, hurried away.

Lockhart added milk and sugar to his coffee, stirred. 'You

really believe Jerome could have sufficient manhood in him to murder Guido?'

'People are not always what they seem to be to others.'

'You would grant the man hidden depths? Let me assure you that his depths are as shallow as his taste in wine.'

Alvarez drank some coffee, replaced it with brandy. 'Of course, if Señor Robertson were to be charged with the murder, inevitably his wife's affair would come to light. Since you are her friend, you would not wish that to happen.'

'You can believe I would risk my bad name by lying to you in a good cause?'

'If that amused you.'

'We understand each other better and better. Jerome never suspected the truth. First, because he dislikes me so much he could never accept the possibility I might have helped to make a fool of him, secondly, because he is so pompously self-satisfied that he's incapable of imagining his wife could cuckold him . . . Does that convince you?'

'It's an opinion I'll bear in mind.'

'Oh, man of little faith! Here am I, trying to help, and you treat me with doubt and even suspicion . . . Let me prove my bona fide. From what Karen has told me and from your talking to me, I gain the certain impression that you are searching for a motive for Guido's death – that is, a stronger one than the natural wish to relieve the world of his presence. Am I right?'

'Perhaps.'

'A furious row would suggest a very antagonistic relationship, would it not?'

'Normally.'

'And a very antagonistic relationship can end in violence?'

'At times.'

'Inspector, if discretion is the better part of criminal investigation, you are a titan in your chosen field.' Lockhart finished his coffee, then his brandy. 'You will have the same again?'

Alvarez saw no reason to refuse.

Lockhart called a waiter across, gave the order. He moved his chair to keep within the shade of the sun umbrella. 'One has to be so careful of the complexion . . . Guido was a man of catholic tastes. I'm sure you appreciate that?'

'It depends on the context.'

'The context of truth. Having met him several times at the ghastly cocktail parties the local, self-declared socialites insist on holding, he suggested I might like to visit his home and enjoy his collection of paintings by modern artists. I asked him if he had any Llulls, and he had two, which does suggest he possessed slightly better taste than his manner suggested. Taste is so important and I decided to accept the invitation. I drove up to his place – could anything be less tasteful? Even if he wasn't responsible for its building, he needn't have lived there – and Inés welcomed me in. I feel certain she's a flighty girl, but why not? Soon, she will be too old to fly. She told me Guido was with a friend and the two men were down by the pool, so why didn't I go down there? The easy manner with which she made the suggestion seemed to negate any possibility that my unscheduled appearance would cause an embarrassment, so that is what I started to do. I was halfway to the pool when it became very obvious that Inés had exaggerated when she had named the visitor a friend. Guido, who was out of sight, was having a furious argument. Rows make me feel very unsafe and I was about to return to my car when he and another man emerged from the poolhouse. When he saw me, he cursed me and accused me of spying. He was beside himself with rage and I became quite trembly. I tried to assure him that far from spying, I was there because of his open invitation to look at his paintings – not etchings, please note – but I might as well have spoken to an olive tree. As you will imagine, my one desire became to extract myself from so invidious a position, so I left. I have always considered self-preservation to be an admirable trait.'

The waiter returned, served them, left. Lockhart stirred sugar into his coffee. 'You do not seem very impressed with my revelation, which I should have expected to arouse great interest.'

'I already knew about the row,' Alvarez answered.

'I should have realized that a man with your talents would

have divined all. Then you even know the identity of the second man?'

'Yes.'

'And he is a suspect?'

'Not exactly a suspect, since the precise nature of the death is not yet established,' Alvarez replied evasively.

'But you agreed that antagonistic relationships often end in violence. Surely here there is motive enough?'

'There are other matters which have to be considered.'

'Your discretion is exasperating.' Lockhart drank. 'I, in my admiration for you, will offer a gem that life has, painfully, taught me. Never trust a man with a downturned moustache: upturned, inventive; downturned, sadistic.'

'I will remember that.'

'Guido's companion had a downturned moustache. Rest assured, he is capable of the vilest outrage without a moment's hesitation.'

Santiago Pons might have a stubbled face when he could not be bothered to shave, but he had never had a moustache.

Lockhart raised his glass and stared at Alvarez over the top of it. 'There seems to have been a shift of emotion. You no longer bear the smug visage of a man who has just been excitedly told what he already knew.'

'Describe the second man.'

'Quite definitely, not my type.'

'Ill-featured?'

'How very percipient. I do find that ugliness casts a cloak over even the most charitable impulses.'

'How old was he?'

'I seldom make that judgement because it's a knife edge between flattery and insult.'

'What was this man's name?'

'I've no idea. There was no graceful introduction.'

'His nationality?'

'I had no way of judging as I did not hear him speak. Since Guido was shouting in gutter Spanish, one must presume he understood the language, if not at such a low level.'

'Are you sure this second man is not a figment of your imagination?'

'Why should I take the trouble to invent him?'

'To divert attention from Señor Robertson.'

'I thought we'd agreed that that was unnecessary? Will a full description satisfy you? Early thirties, slick black hair, dark-brown eyes, ears that stuck out and should have been attended to when young, a thin mouth containing bad teeth under that disgusting moustache – any man of taste eschews unnecessary hair – a pointed chin, a bull neck, and a complete lack of dress sense . . . Is that sufficient?'

'Perhaps too much.'

'What is that supposed to signify?'

'It is very detailed when you saw the man for so short a time.'

'Your suspicions are in danger of becoming a phobia. I always take great note of people's appearances. For instance, although we have not in total enjoyed each other's company for long, I have noticed how your hair is beginning to thin at the crown.'

'It is not,' Alvarez said indignantly.

Lockhart laughed.

CHAPTER 18

As soon as Alvarez arrived at Son Fuyell, Susana and Inés asked him what was to happen to their jobs, and they seemed either not to listen to his answer or else to disbelieve his assertion that he didn't know, because they repeated the question several times. Half an hour passed before he was able to say: 'You know Señor Lockhart, don't you?'

They looked at each other.

'He used to drive Señora Robertson here?'

'The lady who came even though she was married?' Susana sniffed loudly.

'Did he ever arrive on his own?'

'Never,' she said firmly.

'Hang on,' Inés said. 'There was one time.'

'Never!'

'Yes, there was. Don't you remember, you asked the señor for extra time off because your sister was ill and he didn't want to give it to you. The señor was here then.'

'My niece. Such a stupid girl.' The set of her mouth made it clear that she had no intention of explaining the nature of her niece's stupidity.

'When was this?' Alvarez asked.

'Not all that long ago,' Inés answered.

'Margarita was in hospital at the end of last month and the beginning of this,' Susana said.

'Tell me about the time Señor Lockhart came here on his own?'

Inés played with the spoon by the side of her empty mug. 'It's difficult to remember much.'

'Try your best.'

'Well . . . There was a knock on the front door and it was

123

him. Said he'd been invited by the señor whenever he had
the time. I told him, the señor and visitor had just gone
down to the pool and to go there. Wasn't no time before
he was back and left. Can't say I was all that surprised, since
the señor was in such a foul mood. Him and the other man
had been shouting at each other from the start.'

'What was the trouble?'

'How would I know?'

'You might have heard what they were arguing about.'

'In this place, you can hear 'em, but not understand unless
the door's open. And when I took coffee in to 'em in the large
sitting room, they became silent, but from the looks on their
faces, anything could happen.'

'What exactly do you mean by that?'

'Well . . . If they'd started fighting, I wouldn't have been
surprised.'

'You imagine too hard,' Susana said.

'You should've seen them, then you wouldn't talk like
that.'

'What time of day did this other man arrive?' Alvarez
asked.

'The señor had just come down for breakfast.'

'Was the visitor expected?'

'Didn't sound like it when the señor swore like anything
after I told him who had arrived.'

'What was the visitor's name?'

'It was something like . . . Algaba, only it wasn't that.' She
stared across the kitchen table, her sight unfocused. 'Alfaro;
Alfonso; Algarra? . . . Algaro, that's it! Who says I haven't
got a good memory?'

'I do,' answered Susana, 'when it comes to remembering
what needs doing.'

'What about his Christian name?' Alvarez asked.

'Visitors don't tell me that. Unless later on . . .' Inés giggled.

Susana looked disapprovingly at her.

Alvarez briefly wondered just how disturbed Inés had been
by Zavala's approach in the library? Perhaps she'd been more

annoyed than upset, realizing that compliance on her part was most unlikely to lead to her becoming chatelaine of Son Fuyell . . . 'Tell me, d'you think this Algaro was from the island?'

'I'm certain he wasn't. He spoke Castilian and with a terrible accent. Maybe he was from Galicia.'

'Do you think he was a maricón?'

'Are you joking? It was women the señor was interested in.'

'Yet it seems he invited Señor Lockhart to the house.'

The two women looked at each other, doubtful, then surprised. Finally, Inés said: 'These days it seems you can't never be certain until . . .' She stopped when she caught Susana's look.

'Try to describe him.'

'I wouldn't want to be seen with him, that's for sure!'

'Why not?'

''Cause he was uglier than Rodolfo, what works in the bakery.'

'Was he a big man?'

'Depends what you mean by big.'

Showing no impatience, Alvarez continued to question her until satisfied he had heard all she could remember. Her description of Algaro did not closely match Lockhart's description of the man who'd been rowing with Zavala, yet, in part because of the moustache, he had no doubt they were of the same person. Lockhart had been telling the truth and so now there was a fourth suspect . . .

Later, when Alvarez was on the road to Llueso, he called himself a fool. No wonder the name of Algaro had seemed to ring a muffled bell; had he not been a fool, it would have rung a loud peal. Rojas Algaro, the chauffeur who had driven the Jaguar which Bailey claimed had first hit the child.

He sat at his desk and waited, telephone to his ear. Was the superior chief forever too busy to answer the telephone immediately, or did the plum-voiced secretary claim he was in order to bolster his image?

'Yes, what is it?' Salas said, as ever scorning any preliminary and polite greeting.

'It's Inspector Alvarez from Llueso . . .'

'Good God, man, stop wasting my time. I have every reason to know where you're from. What do you want?'

'I have to report a new development in the Zavala case. There is fresh evidence . . .'

'Fresh, or merely uncovered long after it should have been?'

'Señor, until I spoke to Señor Lockhart, I had no reason to know. Inés should, of course, have had the sense to tell me all about the matter initially, but I suppose she didn't stop to realize it might be important; not, of course, that at the time I could have appreciated its true significance . . .'

'Are you incapable of making a short, lucid report? Tell me what happened without all these totally unnecessary asides.'

Alvarez did so.

'You are now claiming there has to be a connection between Algaro's visit and Zavala's death? On what grounds?'

'Considering what happened in England, it would be such a coincidence if there was not one.'

'Coincidences occur all the time.'

'I know they do, but –'

'You have, no doubt, always worked on the principle that common sense plays little part in criminal investigation?'

'Señor, Algaro always drove the Jaguar which Señor Bailey swore overtook him at a dangerous speed and hit the child. Algaro was never questioned by the police because he was able to claim diplomatic immunity, attested to by Señor Zavala. Why would a diplomat protect a chauffeur on false grounds? That was a question never answered. Now we learn that Algaro came to this island and visited Señor Zavala unexpectedly, with the result that there was a violent row. Within a short time, Señor Zavala drowns in circumstances which suggest murder. The sequence of events seems unmistakeable.'

'Only to someone who never questions the obvious.'

'But if the two men were engaged in something they wished to keep secret, the publication of which would have had disastrous consequences for one of them, everything begins to fit.'

'What are you suggesting?'

Alvarez took a deep breath. 'Despite the evidence that Señor Zavala enjoyed many heterosexual relationships, that this was a homosexual one.'

There was a long silence before Salas finally spoke, and when he did, each word was edged with ice. 'Experience should have prepared me to expect that, given the slightest opportunity, you would once again pander to your relish for matters of an objectionable nature.' There was a shorter silence. 'A short while ago, I suggested it would be in your own interests to consult a psychiatrist. Have you done so?'

'No, señor. With great respect, I think you misunderstand the situation. I don't introduce matters you find objectionable because it gives me any pleasure to do so, only because it seems necessary. After all, sex is a large part of people's behaviour.'

'To the few who lack self-control.'

'And I should like to make the point that in these days a homosexual relationship is not viewed by most people as objectionable.'

'The unthinking are easily led and there are always those who seek to destroy the fabric of society by leading them.'

Alvarez stolidly continued. 'Such a relationship would explain many things. While its publication would probably not have harmed Algaro, it might well have harmed Señor Zavala's career if the Bolivian ambassador had been old-fashioned and viewed adversely either the nature of the relationship or that it existed between people of such different rank. Knowing this, Algaro blackmailed Señor Zavala into defending him when he was threatened with being tried in court on the grounds of killing the child.

'Blackmail develops a life of its own. Algaro may initially have intended to employ it only the once, but having found how remunerative it could be, he forced Señor Zavala to give him many sums of money up to the time the other resigned from the diplomatic service. This resignation dramatically altered circumstances because Algaro no longer had the power to blackmail. But later, when he learned Señor Zavala had come to live on this island, he thought he saw the chance to regain the initiative by renewing the relationship. That was why he visited Son Fuyell. To his consternation, Señor Zavala made it clear that he had no intention of agreeing. It does happen that a man whose tastes are both –'

'Refrain from unnecessary details.'

'Algaro, finding his plan had failed, became aggressive and threatened to make their past relationship public on the island.

'It was a feather threat. While one or two of Señor Zavala's more old-fashioned . . . while one or two of his more moral friends might be disturbed by the revelation, most would hold it to be of little account . . .'

'What else can you expect of foreigners?'

'And even those who might be disturbed would hide that fact because wealth always buys acceptance, if not approval. But however useless, the threat aroused Señor Zavala's very explosive temper and he ordered Algaro to clear off in terms that aroused Algaro's bitter resentment to fever pitch.

'From the little I have been able to learn about him, Algaro is probably from a tough environment; when young, he may well have lived in a shanty town around La Paz where violence was the natural way of getting what one wanted. By now, he wanted revenge and so he decided to murder Señor Zavala. But he possesses a degree of cunning and knew that if murder was obvious, his visit to Son Fuyell would be remembered and that could result in his being apprehended before he had time to leave the island, and he set out to make the murder look like accident so that he would have time to escape.'

'Which, if you're right, he will have done, thanks to your inefficiency.'

'It took time to establish the facts . . .'

'Naturally, since it was you who was establishing them.'

'I think now we must ask the Bolivian embassy in London to confirm or deny the possibility of a homosexual relationship between the two men . . .'

'Any such request will be made in your name.'

'We should also ask if Algaro is still in their employ – unlikely, considering the time he must have spent on the island, planning the murder – and if not, what can they tell us about his history and do they have a current address in Bolivia?'

'Is that all?'

'For the moment, señor.'

'Then clearly it has not occurred to you that you are turning assumption into an art form.'

'I don't quite understand. Surely if Señor Zavala was murdered, the guilty man is far more likely to have been someone of Algaro's character than the three we have previously considered as possible suspects?'

'You refer to Algaro's character. Since you admit to having no proof of what that is, you assume. Yet is there a scrap of evidence to negate the possibility that your assumption is rank nonsense? What is there to deny that far from coming from the slums of La Paz, he was born into a family in Santa Cruz well connected in the tin export trade?'

'If so, why would he have been merely a chauffeur at the embassy?'

'It is the mark of muddled thinking to concentrate on irrelevances . . . In a typically blinkered manner, you have failed to do what any efficient investigator does, that is to pursue all possibilities until certain which is of no account. Incredibly, you still cannot confirm whether, or not, Zavala was murdered. There are three men on the island who had a motive for his death, yet you cannot name which motive has the greatest relevance.'

'I have been continuing my investigations . . .'

'Efficiently? Then you can at least now tell me whether any of the three has an alibi which proves beyond doubt that he cannot have murdered Zavala?'

There was a long pause.

'Señor,' Alvarez ventured, 'there has been a great deal of ground which has had to be covered . . .'

'Are you admitting that you have not yet even taken the elementary step of checking the alibis to determine their values?'

Another silence.

'If you feel your abilities have been overtaken by time and progress and you should retire; I shall not dissuade you.' Salas cut the connection.

CHAPTER 19

As Alvarez came to a stop to the side of the lean-to garage of Ca'n Liodre, Fenella, who had been weeding a bed of petunias, stood upright. He stepped out on to the concrete and looked down. 'Good morning, señora.'

'Good morning.' She dropped the hand fork on to the gama grass which surrounded the flower bed, crossed to the steps and climbed these up to the patio. 'Is this a social visit?'

'Unfortunately, not exactly.'

'But that won't prevent your having some coffee?'

'Indeed not.'

'Then sit down while I go inside and make it. Harry's in the village, but he'll be back at any moment.' She went indoors.

He did not immediately sit, but stared above the orange grove at the thin sliver of light which marked as much of the bay as was visible and at the mountains which backed it. There was beauty wherever one went except where it had not had the strength to defy the effect of man's greed.

He sat on one of the patio chairs. It was possible to make out some of the fruit on the nearest orange trees because the sunlight cast shadow which provided shape. In six months, the golden crop would be harvested. Only someone who had eaten an orange newly plucked from a tree enjoyed the true flavour. The ground about the trees had recently been cultivated to destroy weeds. So much land was now being neglected, even if there was enough water to irrigate, because it had become uneconomic to cultivate it. Were he to win El Gordo, he'd buy an estate and run it as it had once been run, every metre of land under cultivation, even if that cost money. It was one of the ironies of life that now one often needed to be wealthy to do what in the past had been done by the poor.

As Fenella returned to the patio, a tray in her hands, the green Astra shooting brake turned the corner of the dirt track to come into sight. 'For once my husband's on time!' she said, as she put the tray down on the table. 'I'll get another mug. I do hope you don't mind a mug?'

He was amused by evidence of yet one more strange habit of the English. What did it matter what anything was served in since it was the contents which were important?

Bailey drove into the garage. A moment later, he walked out and crossed to the table. 'I thought I recognized the car. So how are things going?'

'I think one has to say, slowly, señor.'

'Very appropriate to the climate! I see Fenella's providing coffee, but as yet there is no brandy chaser. Would you like one?'

'Thank you, yes.'

'Shan't be a moment.' He went into the house.

Alvarez allowed the pleasure of relaxation to overcome him to the degree that he was almost asleep when he heard them return.

When the coffee and brandy had been poured out and passed around, Bailey said: 'How can we help you this time?'

'I have to establish one or two facts, señor. The señora is your second wife?'

'Yes.'

Alvarez turned. 'And have you, señora, been married before?'

'What the hell business of yours is that?' Bailey demanded with sudden anger.

'Harry,' she said, 'you know what it's like in this country – apply for a driving licence and they want to know all your great- grandfathers' Christian names.' She turned to face Alvarez. 'My first husband suffered from a serious illness and died not long before I married and came out here to live.'

'Thank you, señora. Señor, before you came to the island,

132

were you convicted of a serious driving offence which resulted in your being sent to jail?'

Bailey's expression showed the shock the question brought. 'Does the past never bury its dead?' he said bitterly.

'Harry,' Fenella murmured as she reached across and put one hand on his. She swung her head round to face Alvarez. 'And if he was? People lied. He should never have been convicted.'

Such loyalty, at the same time defensive and challenging, was only given when a similar loyalty was received. Alvarez knew brief envy – two people who shared strong love possessed a rare prize. 'Señora, the report I read made it clear that if the driver of the Jaguar had been allowed to be questioned, it is unlikely your husband would have been found guilty of more than driving when he had drunk slightly more than the legal limit. The driver of the Jaguar was Rojas Algaro. Señor Zavala was Minister Counsellor for Internal Affairs at the embassy, and it was he who was responsible for Algaro's being provided with diplomatic immunity. When you were at the cocktail party on the second of this month and were introduced to Señor Zavala, no doubt you both failed to realize the part he had played in your lives. But then he boasted about his diplomatic career and you suddenly identified him as the Zavala who had enabled the chauffeur to remain silent. That knowledge was so disturbing that you left the party immediately, without bothering to thank your hostess or explain the reason for your very early departure.'

'Why keep raking up the past?'

'When a man dies in circumstances sufficiently ambiguous to make it uncertain whether his death was accidental or murder, it is necessary to find out if anyone has a motive for his death. If someone did, then it becomes more likely the death was murder, not accident.'

'Are you trying to say that what happened makes for a motive?'

'Only love is sweeter than revenge.'

'You obviously can't understand people.'

'Steady on,' Bailey said.

'I won't. He's got to understand.' She stared intently at Alvarez. 'Harry hates violence and after that dreadful incident when the child was killed, he was physically sick because he could not stop reliving the awful moment when the body brushed his car. Yes, at Dolly's party it was a terrible shock to discover we were talking to the man who was responsible for that ghastly jail sentence; but when we got home, Harry wasn't wild with hatred, he just sat in a chair, remembering, and looking so shattered I wanted to cry . . . He believes that in the end life always evens things up so it's wrong to try to gain revenge. Of course he wished Guido Zavala to hell, but he would never, could never, do anything to help him there. It's utterly ridiculous to think he could have murdered the little rat.'

'His car was seen leaving Son Fuyell that night.'

'No, it wasn't because it couldn't have been. You admitted last time that you couldn't be certain it was his.'

'I think I said I couldn't prove it was. But now, in the circumstances . . .'

'Damn the circumstances. They're wrong.'

'I very much hope so, señora.'

About to say something more, she checked the words. She looked puzzled. 'You sounded as if you really meant that,' she finally said.

'It may sound presumptuous of me, but when I meet two persons like your husband and yourself, it is always my hope that I need never cause either any distress.'

'You're an unusual detective,' Bailey said.

'I accept that as a compliment.'

'As it was meant. You've reassured me that you can understand my wife's somewhat heated defence wasn't intentionally rude.'

'Of course. And for my part, I hope you will understand that I do have to ask you more questions.'

'I can only echo your "of course".'

'Where were you on the evening of the second of this month?'

'He's told you time and again,' Fenella snapped.

'And now I'm going to tell him again,' Bailey said calmly. 'We try never to go out twice on the same day, so having been to Dolly's cocktail party, we were both here, at home.'

'All evening?'

'From when we returned at lunchtime to when we went to bed.'

'Can you prove that that was so?'

'I don't recall anyone's calling to see us, so the answer has to be, no, I can't.'

'Might there have been someone working in the field who could have seen you?' Alvarez indicated the orange grove.

'I've no idea.'

'No one phoned you during the evening?'

'I can't think of anyone who did.'

Fenella said: 'Wendy did.'

'Did she?' Bailey said in surprise. 'Are you sure it was that evening?'

'Yes, because she wanted to know what we thought of Dolly's party and why we'd left early. She asked if you thought the smoked salmon had gone off.'

'Of course! I'd forgotten. Wendy at her most tactless.'

'When did your friend make this call?' Alvarez asked.

'I don't know I can say.' He turned to his wife. 'Have you any ideas?'

'I was gardening, so it was before supper. When did we eat, then? It'll have been before nine.'

'Do you think your friend might be able to be more accurate?' Alvarez asked.

'I suppose it's possible. Parts of Wendy's life are ordered.'

'Perhaps you will give me her name and address?'

Bailey fiddled with his glass. 'This isn't the sort of thing one likes to drag one's friends into.'

'Señor, if she can confirm that the phone call was made within a certain time period, I will know you could not have been at Son Fuyell when Señor Zavala died.'

'Despite the very strong motive and your belief it was my car which was seen?'

'No one can be in two places at once.'

'It's fortunate that our lives aren't governed by quantum mechanics since then supposedly that would be possible . . . Wendy Easton, and she lives in the urbanizacíon halfway down to the puerto . . . What's the name of her place?'

'Casa Blanca,' Fenella replied.

'Typical!'

Alvarez did not understand Bailey's comment until he saw that the house was painted pink. It was a small bungalow and at the foot of the hill so that it lacked any view. Wendy was a generously proportioned woman who suffered the social disadvantage of saying what she thought.

'Why?' she demanded as she stood in the doorway.

A woman of her size, Alvarez thought, really should have the tact not to wear trousers. 'I am carrying out an investigation . . .'

'So you said. What I'm asking is, how can you be so confused as to imagine Harry knows anything?'

'I have to investigate the possibility even if I think it unlikely.'

'Chasing shadows. I suppose you want a drink?'

The abrupt change of conversation, and the aggressive manner in which the question had been put, confused him.

'Do you or don't you?'

'It's not necessary . . .'

'A Mallorquin who has to have his arm twisted before he has a drink? What's the next miracle? A plumber who turns up in less than a month? . . . Are you going to go on standing there?'

Bewildered, he moved forward and she stepped aside – there would not have been room for him to enter had she not done so.

'In there.'

It had been more command than direction. The sitting room was overcrowded with furniture and on one wall was the framed photograph of a man standing by a pony, a polo stick in his hand. Her husband? Army? Had the troops had more cause to beware of her than him?

'What d'you drink? If I haven't got it, you can't have it.'

He asked for a brandy.

She left, to return with a tray on which were bottles, glasses, and a bowl of ice cubes. He watched her pour out two very generous brandies. Most people had their good points to counter their bad ones.

'D'you want soda or ginger with it?'

'If I may, just ice.'

'It's freedom hall.' She dropped four ice cubes into one glass, handed him this, gave herself ginger and ice. She sat.

'Señora, I understand you telephoned Señor and Señora Bailey on the second of this month, in the evening.'

'Did I?'

'You don't remember?'

'Should I?'

'I was hoping you would.'

'Hopes come cheaply.'

'You asked him what he thought of a cocktail party you'd both been to.'

She drank. 'That's right! Dolly's. A silly woman, all lipstick and scent. At her age, she should have grown out of such things.'

'You spoke to Señor Bailey?'

'That sounds logical, since he answered the phone. Fenella was gardening. Can't think why they don't employ someone to do that. Not, of course, that any of the locals know what a proper garden is.'

'Did you discuss anything else?'

'I asked him why he'd left early – was he or Fenella ill?'

'What did he answer?'

'Can't remember. Some waffle or other. He's far too tactful to tell the truth. I'll swear the smoked salmon was off. Probably kept from the last party. Dolly's as rich as Croesus and behaves like Scrooge.' She belched. When she saw his expression, she said: 'Better out than in, whether you're a duchess or a lavatory attendant.' She opened a heavily carved wooden box, picked out a cheroot. 'Do you use these?'

'I prefer cigarettes.'

137

'I'm not going to offer you one because I don't have any.'

He lit a cigarette as she lit her cheroot. 'Señora, can you say what the time was when you phoned Señor Bailey?'

'Good God, you think I can be bothered to watch a clock?'

'You have no idea when you made the call?'

'Must have been before nine. After nine, everyone's too sloshed to talk sense.'

Since she had already finished her drink, he thought that it was, at least in her case, a correct assumption.

As if in response to his thoughts, she stood. 'What's the matter with the brandy? Not to your refined taste?'

He drained his glass and handed it to her. 'Can you be more exact about the time?'

She crossed to the tray, on a small glass-topped table, and refilled the two glasses. As she handed him his, she said: 'If I'm on my own, I always watch the news at eight.' She returned to her chair and sat, so energetically that some of the drink slopped over the top of the glass and on to her hand. She transferred the glass to her left hand, licked her right one. 'Waste not, want not . . . I'll probably have rung during the first break for commercials. Bloody things! I make certain I never buy anything advertised on television.'

'Roughly when would that break be?'

'Didn't I say, I don't watch the clock?'

'This was English television?'

'You think I watch the Spanish news?'

It would be easy to find out when the commercial breaks normally occurred on the English service, but it was reasonable to assume it would be around a quarter past the hour. Since Bailey had been at home at that time, he could not have been anywhere near Son Fuyell when Zavala died, and the green Astra shooting brake was an irrelevance. He was glad.

CHAPTER 20

When Alvarez climbed out of his car, a single puffball cloud, drifting eastwards, held him in its shade for almost a minute as he stood still. When once more in sharp sunlight, he crossed to the patio of Ca'n Ibron. As he climbed the steps, Pons came through the doorway. 'Looking at you, I thought you'd died on your feet,' was his greeting.

'I was thinking how things change from light to dark and back again.'

'Are you boozed out of your mind?'

'No.'

'You talk like you are.'

'Never judge a lamb by the way it bleats.'

'It's a long time since you were a lamb, that's for bloody sure! What do you want now?'

'I've some questions.'

'You still think I did the bastard in?'

'You'd certainly have enjoyed doing it.'

'There's a lot of things I'd enjoy doing, but ain't done.'

There was a pause.

'Shall we sit?' Alvarez finally said.

'Tired out after too long a siesta?'

'I've been too busy working to sleep.'

'More likely too busy sleeping to work.'

Alvarez crossed to one of the patio chairs and sat.

'Make yourself at home! And now I suppose you want some booze you've not had to pay for?'

'That makes it taste better.'

Pons went indoors and shouted, returned to sit on the opposite side of the table.

'How are the olives looking?' Alvarez asked.

'It's going to be a poor crop.'

Crops were always going to be poor – the gods of the harvest did not like boasters.

'But there'll be enough?'

'Enough for what?'

'There's nothing to compare with the taste of the first pressing.'

'Which'll stay here, so don't waste your time coming round at the end of the year to ask how I am.'

'A suspicious mind makes for a poor digestion.'

'It makes certain it's my digestion what's poor and not yours.'

Cristina came out of the house. Plainly nervous, she did not look at Alvarez as she greeted him before putting the tray down on the table.

'He's on the scrounge again,' Pons said. 'Wants some oil when it's harvested.'

'I was merely asking what sort of crop you'll be likely to have,' Alvarez protested.

'Paid to sit on his backside and do nothing all day, and when he does move, it's to come here scrounging.'

'Don't you think . . .' she began, stopped when there was a sound from inside. 'Is that Lucía . . . I must go.' She hurried back inside.

'She worries,' Pons said. 'Always expecting the kids to get into trouble.'

'Like the adults?'

'What's that supposed to mean?'

'That three jacks never were worth betting one's shirt on.'

'You'd dance on a man's grave, given the chance.' He poured out two brandies, pushed a glass across the table.

Alvarez helped himself to three cubes of ice. The fountain was casting a shadow that, with only a little imagination, formed the profile of a very old man with a crooked nose. A quick movement on the patio roof was a gecko, which 'froze' when he looked up at it. A small blue butterfly settled briefly on a nearby rose bush. An overflying aeroplane left a trail in the sky, the four streams merging into two, the two into one, the one gradually disappearing. A kestrel appeared, hovered, swept away to the right. A dog barked, several others responded, all became silent. Swallows performed aerial acrobatics . . . 'If this were my place, I'd do anything to keep hold of it.'

'It ain't yours.'

'If you'd decided to kill Zavala, how would you have gone about that?'

'With an axe.'

'That's what I reckoned.'

They drank.

'If I tell you Zavala died at around eight o'clock that night, where would you have been at the time?'

'Here.'

'Not drinking in one of the bars to forget?'

'Any more suggestions and I'll see where my axe is.'

'It just seems odd for someone like you to be at home in the evening.'

Pons drained his glass. 'Can't you get this into your rock-solid head? When I had to tell Cristina what had happened, I swore to her I wouldn't act stupid again. And I ain't. I've been at home every night.'

'But you can't prove to me that you were here the night Zavala died?'

Pons turned round to face the front door and shouted. Seconds later, Cristina hurried out of the house. 'It's all right,' she said as she came to a stop by the table. 'Lucía banged her arm, but she's not really hurt.'

Despite his present, pressing concerns, Pons said: 'Are you sure she's not broken anything?'

'There's hardly a bruise.' She looked quickly at Alvarez, then away. 'All she did was tumble over a toy that was left lying around . . . D'you want something to eat?'

'I'm not feeding the lazy sod as well as boozing him.'

She drew in her breath with an audible hiss. 'You mustn't talk like that.'

'It's the only language he understands.'

'But he's a policeman.'

'Wasn't up to anything else.'

141

'Santi, please . . .' She did not finish.

Alvarez smiled. 'Between friends, rudeness becomes affection.'

'Not with me it don't,' Pons said. 'Not when I keep telling him I've been here every evening and couldn't have done the bastard in and he won't believe me.'

'Won't you sit down?' Alvarez asked. 'I'd like a word.'

'I do the asking in my house,' Pons shouted.

'But it takes you time to remember?'

Pons used a few of the expressions which made Mallorquin so rewarding a language in which to swear.

Cristina hastily sat.

Alvarez quietly asked her: 'Can you remember Tuesday, the second of this month?'

'Yes.'

It was so obviously a lie. She would lie to the devil, he thought admiringly, if that would help her family. 'How can you be so certain of the date?'

'I just am.'

'One evening's very much like another, especially when one's talking about almost a month ago.'

'What are you after?' Pons demanded. 'Ask her a question and she answers it and then you try to tell her she can't know what she's talking about.'

'I have to try to confirm everything.'

'Then confirm this. She remembers I was here that evening.'

'I haven't heard her say that.'

'Bloody deaf as well as thick?' Pons spoke to his wife. 'I was here all that evening, wasn't I?'

'Yes,' she answered.

'Why can you place that evening for certain?' Alvarez asked.

Pons, finding action easier than words, slammed a thick fist down on the table, making the glasses jump and the little ice left in them jingle against their sides.

She spoke very quickly. 'He hasn't gone out any evening since he told me about losing all that money. I swear that's the truth. You must believe me. Why won't you?'

'A good wife always supports her husband, whatever the truth.'

142

'You think I'm lying?'

'Regretfully, I have to consider the possibility.'

'Then I suppose you believe we'll have taught the children to lie as well?'

'The children?'

Her tone was now challenging. 'If they say Santiago has been at home every evening for weeks, will you tell them they're liars?'

'Of course not.'

She stood, went over to the open doorway, and called. Rosa and Lucía came out on to the patio. Rosa said hullo to Alvarez, Lucía, far more shy, did not.

'The inspector wants to ask you something,' Cristina said. 'You're to tell him everything you can because we want to help him. Do you understand?'

Rosa said she did, Lucía remained silent.

Cristina faced Alvarez. 'Well?'

He wondered how to question them without upsetting, perhaps even frightening, them? He cleared his throat. He picked up his glass and drained it. He decided he'd rather talk to Salas than do what he was trying to do now . . .

Cristina brought an end to his problem. 'Where does Daddy go in the evenings?'

'He's here,' Rosa answered.

'What does he do when he's here?'

'Everything. He built the treehouse and Lucía tried to knock it down . . .'

'I didn't,' Lucía protested.

With a skill that Alvarez admired, Cristina gradually encouraged them to confirm what he had already been told. In the long past, Pons had seldom been at home in the evenings and very rarely had he kissed them good night; but for ages now he had played with them, built them the lovely treehouse, kissed them good night. Every night. Every, every night. Not one had been missed . . .

She hugged them, said that they deserved a chocolate biscuit each for being so clever, and led them indoors.

'Is that good enough for you?' Pons asked aggressively.

143

For children, yesterday was a long time ago, a month, an almost forgotten age. Yet they were sharply aware of unwelcome changes. So whilst it was certain they could not have picked out July the second and named anything specific which had happened on that day, they had become used to their father's always being at home in the evenings and so had there been one when he had not been, it seemed probable they would have remembered that fact. Cristina had made not the slightest effort to prompt them; each had been certain that for weeks and weeks and weeks, their father had been at home all evening . . .

'Are you going to call 'em liars like you've been calling me and Cristina?' Pons demanded.

'I haven't done that.'

'You're a bloody liar!'

'Perhaps. They say one has to walk a long way to find a completely truthful man.'

'A long way from where you're standing, that's for sure.'

There was a silence. Finally, Alvarez said: 'How are things at work?'

'There's a job or two around since the Germans are back.'

He was glad to hear that. Since all Germans were known to be wealthy, Pons would inflate his estimates to add a hidden profit. Hopefully, the extra money would enable him to save his home and his business and good would follow a small malpractice. A moralist might condemn, a pragmatist would applaud.

Alvarez fingered his glass to draw attention to the fact that it was empty.

CHAPTER 21

Dominica opened the front door of Ca'n Jerome. 'You again!' she said, in a friendly voice. 'What's it this time?'

'I'd like a word with Señor Robertson,' Alvarez answered as he stepped into the hall.

'There won't be many who'll say that!'

He smiled. 'Is he in?'

'He is, shouting for this and that, as if he'd no legs or arms. What he needs is a couple of slaves.'

'And is the señora here?'

'She's out shopping with her boyfriend.'

'Boyfriend?'

'Only in a manner of speaking. With Señor Lockhart. Makes me laugh, he does. And the life he leads is his own affair. I don't hold with the way the señor talks about him behind his back.'

'Doesn't like him?'

'Doesn't like anyone but himself, if you ask me.'

'Where is he right now?'

'By the pool, moaning and drinking.'

Alvarez went through the sitting room and out on to the covered patio where Robertson sat in a luxurious pool chair by the side of a table on which were bottles, ice container, and one glass. 'Good morning, señor.'

'What the hell do you want?'

'I'm sorry to bother you, but I should like to ask a few questions.'

'I'm too ill.'

'I am very sorry to hear that.'

'The doctors can't find out what's wrong.'

'Sadly, it can be difficult.'

'Impossible, when everyone's incompetent.'

'Señor, would you mind if I sat?'

There was no answer.

Alvarez sat. He studied the bottles on the table, but the hint was not accepted.

'What is it, then?'

'As I'm sure you'll appreciate, I have to ask certain questions which may give offence if the reason for them is misunderstood.'

'I don't understand what you're talking about.'

'It could seem I'm suspicious of the person to whom the question is put; but in truth, it is only asked in order to make certain that I can confirm innocence.'

'It's a pity you can't speak understandable English.'

'I fear I can only do my best.'

'That's what the damned doctors keep saying. Doesn't help when the best is no bloody good.'

'Señor Zavala died on the second of this month . . .'

'Good God, have you barged in here to go through all that again?'

'The medical evidence suggested he died between seven and nine in the evening. I am asking people if they can prove where they were at those times on that day in order to be certain they can know nothing about Señor Zavala's death.'

'Why come here and make a nuisance of yourself?'

'I should like to make certain that you could not have been involved.'

'Are you trying to suggest I might?'

'You perhaps had cause to dislike him?'

'No one liked him. He covered himself in so much scent you could smell him a mile away.'

'And that was not preferable to the alternative?'

'In my country, men smell like men, not women. Leastwise, that's how it used to be. But the country's gone to hell; everyone wanting two holidays a year and all the wrong people making money. Where's it all going to end, that's what I'd like to know.'

146

'It is possible, in a happier nation. Señor, did you ever wonder why your wife was so friendly with Señor Lockhart? Have you ever had reason to disapprove of the friendship?'

'What the hell do you think? I've told her often enough that it doesn't do our image any good to be seen with the likes of him, but she can't see that. Just keeps saying he's so amusing. When I was younger, his kind wasn't thought amusing.'

'You've never seen any other reason to object to the friendship?'

'That's none of your business.'

'I'm afraid it is.'

'The last time you were here, you tried to act as if you could give orders. I'm not putting up with all that again. Clear off.'

'Señor, have you ever had reason to object to your wife's friendship with Señor Lockhart, other than on the grounds of the type of person he is?'

'Are you going to get out?'

'Only after you have answered my questions.'

'If you're here in ten seconds' time, I'll tell the maid to get the gardener to throw you out.'

'You do not seem to understand that since I am carrying out an investigation, I am entitled to ask whatever questions I wish. If you continue to refuse to answer them, I will have you brought to the post in Llueso where you will stay until you change your mind.'

'Are you threatening to lock me up?'

'Only if that becomes necessary.'

'Don't you understand I'm English?'

'Unfortunately for you, that does not prevent your being restrained.'

Robertson drained his glass. He poured himself another drink.

'Do you intend to help me, señor?'

'I don't remember what the question was,' he blustered.

'I'm sure that you do.'

Robertson drank.

'I'm sorry, señor, but since you insist on refusing to . . .'

Robertson's manner suddenly became conciliatory. 'I've never had any other reason . . . The thing is, she's a bit younger than me and still likes going around. I can't take her everywhere because I'm not fit enough and so in a way it's good her going with him because I can be certain he won't try anything. Not that she'd ever respond. She's totally loyal. I know people think there are problems when there's a little difference in ages, but it's never been like that for us.'

'She has not been friendly with any other man?'

A little of Robertson's belligerence returned. 'Haven't I just said so?'

'She was not seeing Señor Zavala before he died?'

'Of course she wasn't. How dare you ask such a question.'

Alvarez would have liked to shatter the other's stupid, bombastic attitude, to make him realize that there was no fool like a complacent fool, but he would never willingly cause pain to any man, even one who treated him with rude contempt. 'It is a question which had to be put, señor. Earlier, I said I needed to know for certain where people were at the time of Señor Zavala's death. Will you tell me where you were?'

'It's a hell of a long time ago.'

'Does that mean you cannot be certain?'

'No, it doesn't. It'll be a damned sight easier if you leave me to say what I mean. Since it was the evening, I was here, unless we were out for dinner.'

'Would you have made a note of any such invitation?'

'Naturally we keep a social diary.'

'Please look at it and see if you were with friends that evening.'

Robertson seemed about to refuse, but then he emptied his glass, stood – to the accompaniment of many groans – and went indoors. When he returned, he had a small diary. He sat, opened the diary, flicked through the pages, found the one he wanted. 'We hadn't a dinner party that night. I had to go and see a specialist at the Playa Neuva hospital and that was a complete waste of time!'

'Do you know the specialist's name?'

'I can't remember. They've all got ridiculous names.'

'You've no idea?'

'Maybe it was something like Canals.'

Alvarez stood. 'Thank you for all your help, señor.' He managed not to sound too sarcastic. As he walked away, Robertson poured himself another drink; passing through the sitting room, Alvarez imagined velvet-smooth, ice-cool brandy comforting his parched throat . . .

A BMW drove in and stopped by the side of the Ibiza. By the time he had descended the steps to the drive, Karen was out of the BMW. She hurried round the bonnet. 'What are you doing here?' she demanded breathlessly.

She wore a white blouse and underneath almost certainly no brassière; the pink-coloured trousers could hardly have hugged her shapely hips and smoothly rounded bottom with greater care. Even though he knew her to be a bitch, even though he could be certain she regarded him as too old to be remotely interesting, he could not prevent his mind supposing. Small wonder that, when in despair after his mistress had deserted him, Miguel Cuñelles had written: In the presence of a desirable woman, every man is weak. 'I have been speaking with your husband, señora.'

'What about?'

Lockhart spoke through his opened window. 'Be careful, sweetie. Remember my warning about the shy, sly, self-effacing inspector.'

She ignored him. 'What have you been saying to Jerome?'

Alvarez answered her. 'I asked if he could tell me where he was on the evening of the second of this month.'

'Why?'

'To learn if I could confirm that he knew nothing about the death of Señor Zavala.'

'Or that perhaps he knew everything?' Lockhart suggested.

Karen swung round. 'For God's sake, shut up.' She turned back. 'What did he tell you?'

Alvarez said: 'That he consulted a specialist at the Playa Neuva hospital.'

149

'That was all?'

'He did also mention his firm belief that you were not seeing Señor Zavala before his death.'

'Why should he say that? You must have asked him and made him suspicious. You sod!'

'Señora, I merely asked if you had been friendly with the señor and he said that you had not because – I could not quite follow the reasoning – Señor Zavala used rather a lot of perfume.'

'You didn't tell him . . . You know . . .'

'He clearly believes such a possibility to be impossible.'

'Oh! . . . I'm sorry about what I said a moment ago. It was just me being really stupid. You're far too nice and kind to have told him.'

Ironically, he preferred her when she was not trying to be pleasant and was not hiding her disinterested scorn.

'You can breathe again,' Lockhart said.

'You're not half as amusing as you think!' Her tone was shrill. She spoke to Alvarez once more. 'You're certain he doesn't believe that . . .' She became silent.

'I am as certain as I can be,' Alvarez assured her.

'You've been very kind and I really do appreciate that . . . I'd better go and see how he is. He said he wasn't feeling at all well, but as Dominica was there, I thought it safe to leave him just for a little while.'

'Who could doubt your concern?' Lockhart asked.

She smiled at Alvarez, ignored Lockhart, crossed to the steps and climbed them, took a key out of her handbag and unlocked the front door, went inside after a quick good-bye wave.

'I trust you admire her as much as I do?' Lockhart said.

'She offers cause for admiration?' Alvarez asked.

'That's unworthy of you. It makes you sound small-minded and not the broad-minded, perspicacious inspector you so clearly are. Of course she must be admired. Hasn't she pulled the wool over her husband's eyes, despite his advantage of a coarse and illiberal mind. She might have gone far if –'

'If Señor Zavala had lived?'

'Not necessarily. But he could have been the catalyst. As I've said many times to her, she was being naively optimistic when she believed Guido would have her on her terms. He was a man for whom the chase was more piquant than the consummation; he would never have found any difficulty in casting her off when that seemed an advantageous thing to do. She just refused to admit that he might do to her what he had done to so many other women. Desire blinds, does it not, Inspector?'

'I've no idea.'

'I might believe you, with your sad expression, if I had not watched you visually stalk her as she crossed from here to the house.'

About to deny the allegation indignantly, Alvarez checked the words – that was the reaction Lockhart sought. 'We have a saying, A candle is not finished until the wick is gone even if it gives little light.' He changed the conversation. 'What have you and the señora been doing this morning?'

'Shopping.'

'The señora carried no parcels or bags into the house; there are none lying on the seats of your car.'

'What an observant person you can be!'

'Is she, with your connivance, already meeting another man?'

'Why should you consider that possible?'

'You have an air of self-satisfaction.'

Lockhart laughed. 'I can't tell you how pleasant conversation with you is.'

'Is she seeing another man?'

'Is the answer of any consequence to your present investigation?'

'I can't tell until I know the answer.'

'Then let it remain no more than a possibility. The art of living a full life is to be uncertain about everything but other people's ages . . . Nothing could brighten my day more than for you to drive down to the port and continue our conversation over a few drinks in my flat.'

'I'm very busy.'

'Small reason to deny me the pleasure of your company or to deny yourself the pleasure of some Gran Reserva Osborne, a brandy that challenges all but the truly great cognacs.'

He was awoken by the last trump. 'What's up?' he asked hoarsely, expecting the four horsemen to gallop through the bedroom.

Dolores banged on the door of his bedroom again. 'If you don't hurry up and move, you won't get to the office before it's time to come back.'

Which seemed the perfect reason for remaining where he was. But the superior chief might ring, ostensibly in search of information, in reality to check that his inspector was at work. Doubting Thomas could have learned a thing or two from Salas.

'The coffee's cold because you didn't come down on time.'

She could make fresh. He sat up and wished he had not, as pain streaked through his head and he became aware of a taste in his mouth that went beyond description . . . Lockhart had tried to drink him under the table. In the event, it had been Lockhart who had ended up wide to the world, sprawled out in a chair, head lolling back, mouth open . . . Hopefully, if he awoke, he would feel so ill that never again would he be stupid enough to try to out-drink a Mallorquin . . .

As Alvarez entered the kitchen, Dolores said: 'I shall never understand how men can be such fools.'

He slumped down on the chair by the table.

'They drink until they boast what great hidalgos they are, then act like cockroaches when their heads ache and their stomachs revolt.'

'Do you mind?' he murmured plaintively.

'I mind very much. You will remember what happened at lunch?'

He struggled to recall the past and failed.

'Clearly it is nothing to you that I slave all morning to cook the meal! It is not even of passing account that I sacrifice my life trying to please. Being a man – and sometimes, as now, something less than a man – you are only concerned with yourself.'

He struggled to stem the flood. 'I never stop thinking how wonderful you are. I respect you . . .'

'I will remind you how much you respect me. So much that when I serve Bacalla a la Mallorquina – cooked to perfection – you say it looks like yesterday's Ous de Soller and laugh at such wit!'

It was impossible he could have acted so crassly.

'So! So despite so gross and ignorant an insult, I shall not stop cooking because a woman's life is determined as a burden and she cannot escape her fate. But mark this well, Enrique Alvarez. Never again will I seek a special dish, never again will I work myself into an early grave to cook it, since those who will eat are incapable of appreciating what I have provided. Your chosen pleasure is to swill yourself stupid and to mock.'

'You can't understand . . .'

'It is you who has to understand that I am no longer prepared to be a slave.' Head held high, she crossed to the bead curtain and passed through it.

The coffee was cold. There was no coca, not even a stale slice. His head was thumping like a runaway engine and the taste in his mouth had worsened. The present was bleak enough, but if Dolores held to her threats, the future was going to be unbearable.

The receptionist in the hospital suggested that a doctor with a name like Canal was probably Dr Canellas. Alvarez walked along a couple of corridors and sat down on one of the chairs set outside the consulting room. His thoughts became ever bleaker. Dolores, prone to exaggeration, often threatened trouble, but seldom wrought it. Yet this time, she had sounded like someone determined to carry out what she said. If only women possessed a developed sense of humour . . .

The nearest door opened and a nurse looked out. 'Inspector Alvarez.'

He stood, carefully. He entered a room that contained an

examination bed, equipment that would have scared him had he looked at it and imagined its uses, and a desk at which a doctor sat. He introduced himself.

'So what's your trouble?' The doctor visually examined Alvarez with professional interest.

'There's nothing wrong with me.'

'No?'

'I need to know if someone is a patient of yours and if he is, to find out something.'

'You are asking me to ignore medical confidentiality?'

'No, of course not. The problem isn't medical. It's whether you can confirm a certain person consulted you?'

'Who is he?'

'Señor Jerome Robertson.'

Canellas's manner changed and became more friendly. 'That name sounds familiar.' He turned to the nurse. 'That's right, isn't it?'

She giggled.

'Inspector, without breaking any confidences, I can confirm that he is one of my patients, despite his frequently expressed opinion that I am no more competent than many of my colleagues on the island.'

'Did you see him on the second of this month?'

'It is quite probable. He is a frequent visitor.'

'Would it be possible to check?'

Canellas spoke to the nurse. 'Check through appointments for the inspector.' He looked at Alvarez. 'I'm a very busy man.'

Alvarez accepted the curt dismissal and stood. He had hurriedly to reach for the back of the chair for support.

Canellas studied him with renewed interest. 'Are your hands beginning to shake? Do you find you're having difficulty in balancing?'

'I just tripped over my own feet.'

'Because you are unable to lift them?'

'Nothing like that. Thank you for your help.' Alvarez hurried out of the room. Were his hands beginning to shake from time to time; was he occasionally having difficulty in

154

balancing; had his feet become clumsily heavy? Had the doctor discerned the symptoms of some fatal illness which until then had been hidden from himself? He could have asked. But it would have needed a braver man than he to do so.

The nurse stepped out into the corridor. 'Señor Robertson had an appointment on the second of the month.'

'At what time?'

'Seven-thirty. But I remember that the doctor was held up by a sick patient and he could not see Señor Robertson immediately. The señor complained about that. Even for a foreigner, he is a rude and arrogant man.'

'How long d'you think he had to wait?'

'Not nearly as long as he said. Perhaps half an hour.'

'And he would have been in consultation for maybe another half-hour?'

'Probably a little less than that.'

So now the only suspect was Algaro.

CHAPTER 22

On Saturday morning, Salas was in an ill-tempered mood. 'You realize the import of what you're saying?'

'I think so,' Alvarez replied carefully.

'You are admitting that in the course of a month you have failed to reach any firm conclusion.'

'It's not quite as long as that . . .'

'You would quibble over a single day?'

Superiors could be pedantic; juniors could not quibble. 'Señor, the time has not been wasted.'

'That is a matter of opinion. You are convinced Zavala was murdered and did not drown by accident, but cannot produce a single piece of evidence to substantiate your claim. You name Algaro the murderer, but cannot prove that this is so.'

'The trouble is that so many of the facts are ambiguous . . .'

'Ambiguity resides in untidy minds.'

'But it's proved impossible to be certain about so many things. What happened to the glass that went missing from the poolhouse? Was it moved because it had fingerprints on it? Or was it previously broken because it had been accidentally dropped, yet Inés did not know this? Is she even correct in saying that it went missing that day? It's easy to be wrong about such things.'

'Who can be in a better position to remark on that?'

'Then there is the bruise on the dead man's throat. The medical evidence is that this was occasioned with no great force so it could have been accidental. And there can be no certainty that the wound to the head occurred after the blow to the throat . . .'

'Do you intend endlessly to discuss each piece of evidence?'

'I'm trying to explain why there's so much ambiguity.'

'Yet despite this, you are prepared to name Algaro the murderer?'

'If Señor Zavala was murdered.'

Salas sighed heavily: 'Comisario Hornas once said to me that after speaking to you for only a couple of minutes, he began to lose his grip on reality.'

'He found great difficulty in understanding Mallorquin customs . . .'

'Hardly to be wondered at.'

'There are many on the Peninsula which seem strange to us . . .'

'Kindly refrain from pointless digressions.'

'Señor, we will know if Señor Zavala was murdered when we question Algaro. There was clearly an unusual relationship between him and Señor Zavala, perhaps explicable only if . . .'

'You will not indulge in unwholesome speculation.'

'Whatever form this relationship took, it continued after Señor Zavala left the diplomatic service and came to live on this island. Whether there were many or few meetings between the two men, we don't know, but we can be certain that there was one at which Señor Zavala, notoriously fiery-tempered, became very angry. A bitter disagreement provides a further motive for murder. Prolonged and detailed investigation – which, as you will know, always takes a great deal of time – has convinced me that none of the three initial suspects murdered Señor Zavala. This leaves only Algaro. When we have questioned him about the relationship and the cause of the row, we will, I am certain, identify his motive. Then, when he cannot provide an alibi, we will know he murdered Señor Zavala.'

'I don't think I have ever before listened to such a chain of illogical presumptions. You claim that because there was a row, Zavala's death must have been murder; because it was murder, the row was obviously bitter enough to confirm motive.'

'I don't think that's quite what I was saying, señor. Perhaps if I go over the facts in more detail . . .'

'God forbid!' Salas said before he cut the connection.

Alvarez settled back in the chair. There were times when the world was grey merging into black. Supper the previous night had been no more than an apology of a meal, yet Dolores had rubbed salt into their wounds by asking them if they'd enjoyed it. Naturally, they'd replied that it had been delicious – one did not jab a fighting bull in the ribs – at which she had said that that was good and she would cook more meals like it. After she'd cleared the table and was washing up, Jaime had leaned across the table and in a whisper said it was all his fault and just what in the hell was he going to do about the impossible situation? To which, of course, there could be no answer . . .

He was about to leave to go to the Club Llueso for a much needed merienda when the phone rang. Inexplicably, he answered the call instead of ignoring it.

'The superior chief,' said the superior chief's secretary in her plum-laden voice, 'has asked me to inform you that a communication has been received from the Bolivian embassy in London. I shall fax this to you as soon as this call is over. When you have read the information, you are to ring the superior chief, before midday since he has to leave the office to attend an important conference. Is that clear?'

'Yes, señorita.'

He did not have time to say goodbye before she rang off. Life was ever unfair. When you were a superior chief, you could stop work early in order to enjoy an extra round of golf; when you were a mere inspector, you had to work all hours even on a Saturday.

He went downstairs and collected the fax, did not bother to read it before leaving the building and making his way to the club, where, at the sight of him, the barman poured out a large brandy and set a scoop of coffee in the machine.

He sat at an empty table. Saturday lunch was usually a feast, but today it might be no more than they had had the previous evening; it was conceivable that it might even be worse . . .

'Cheer up,' said the barman as he put a cup of coffee on

158

the table, 'you may be dead by tomorrow and then all your troubles will be over.'

He drank most of the brandy and tipped what remained into the coffee, took the glass to the bar for a refill. 'Drowning your sorrows?' said the barman.

'Eating them.'

He returned to the table and drank the second brandy, and a little of the greyness lightened. He remembered the fax and brought the creased sheet of paper out of his pocket. Rojas Algaro had ceased to work at the embassy and had returned to Bolivia. Records showed he was unmarried and his last known address was in Sucre.

The next paragraph had been headed 'Confidential' and the word had been underlined twice.

There had never been any suggestion of a homosexual relationship between Zavala and Algaro and the former's reputation was as a ladies' man. However, Zavala had granted Algaro diplomatic immunity when the latter had seemingly been involved in a serious traffic offence in Halfchurch. Questioned about his action, Zavala had stated that Algaro had come to him and sworn that he knew nothing about the fatal accident and that the other driver was lying; had appealed for his help in escaping what would be a terrible miscarriage of justice. Believing Algaro to be truthful, Zavala had decided to do what he could, which had been to act beyond his authority. When his action had become known, the matter had been referred to the ambassador who had held that in the circumstances, publicly to admit that a senior member of the embassy had lied in order to protect an employee from criminal action would reflect such dishonour on the embassy, and therefore the nation, that this could not be allowed. No denial of diplomatic immunity would be issued. The ambassador's ruling had caused considerable disagreement, but had had to be accepted. He had ordered both men to hand in their resignations.

Some months later, two women on a flight from La Paz were stopped at Heathrow airport and searched; each was found to be carrying cocaine internally. When questioned, both had refused to name any of their contacts. Later, however, in the hopes of obtaining a lighter sentence, one of them had claimed that until recently their contact had been an employee at the Bolivian embassy. When the embassy was notified of this allegation, they had issued a very strong denial. However, one of the chauffeurs, reprimanded for insolence to a Peruvian visitor, said that Algaro had been engaged in the drug trade. No proof of this assertion had been uncovered.

Drugs. The key that unlocked the puzzle. And how right he'd been to suggest that Zavala had been murdered by Algaro, following the row at Son Fuyell! He emptied his glass, stood, crossed to the bar and asked for a refill.

'It's lucky we're not suffering a crime wave,' said the bartender.

Alvarez drummed on the desk with the fingers of his right hand as he waited, receiver to his left ear. How did he play the scene? Arrogantly, pointing out that in the face of so much doubt, he had been right to persevere? Tactfully, accepting that because there had been lack of hard proof, it had been right not to agree that the possible was probable? Delicately, offering the view that when circumstances seemed to paint one picture . . .

'Yes?' said Salas.

'It's Inspector Alvarez . . .'

'Do you announce yourself because you suffer from a mistaken sense of importance?'

'Only because I can't be certain your secretary has told you who's calling, señor.'

'Naturally, I have an efficient secretary. Well?'

'The fax from the Bolivian embassy does appear to confirm a special relationship between Señor Zavala and Algaro, though not based on homosexuality . . .'

'Much to your salacious disappointment, no doubt.'

'Señor, the circumstances being what they were . . .'

'Whatever the circumstances, an uncorrupted mind does not choose to leap to a corrupted conclusion.'

'The facts . . .'

160

'As I suggested, their relationship was always likely to have had a financial basis.'

'I'm sorry, but I don't remember your saying that.'

'A good memory is a prerequisite to efficient detection. Which undoubtedly explains why it has taken you over a month to uncover what should have been apparent almost from the beginning.'

'It's only because I questioned many people, have checked every fact, that Algaro's connection with the case ever came to light . . .'

'Excuses denote inefficiency. What do you propose now? Or is it unrealistic to expect you to have considered how to proceed from this point?'

'I suggest we request the Bolivian authorities to trace Algaro's present address, explaining why we should like to question him.'

'Naturally that has already been done.'

'Then for the moment there does not seem to be anything more to do.'

'A judgement quickly conceived and gratefully accepted?'

'Señor, it is only Algaro who can answer the unanswered questions . . .'

Salas cut the connection.

Alvarez settled back in the chair. Dolores was a woman of strong emotions and even stronger will, and she suffered from the female inability of being unable to overcome resentments, even petty ones; but where the family was concerned, she could be weak. If he bought a bunch of flowers on the way home and presented this to her on the excuse that he thought it was Mother's Day and he wished to salute the finest of mothers, would she not be so warmed by his loving thoughtfulness that while lunch could not be changed, supper might be a golden meal?

Supper was a kind of stew; the kind that made those eating it hesitate to identify the contents. And if that were not cruelty enough, she claimed to have forgotten to buy more wine and there was only one bottle between them.

161

Jaime poured himself another brandy, added ice. He looked carefully in the direction of the bead curtain before he said: 'Alejo's old woman took it out on him for a whole month after he was caught with the girl from Mestara.'

'He was a fool to let himself be caught,' Alvarez said.

'It was bad luck. How could he expect his wife to go out and pick tomatoes in the middle of the afternoon?'

'Women never do what's expected of 'em.'

'Suppose . . . suppose Dolores is so pig-headed that she decides to go on being bloody silly for longer than a month?'

'She won't. Being caught having a piece on the side is one thing, making a joke about the grub doesn't compare.'

'Not to you, maybe, but what about her? She's made us starve for a week already. What's to say it won't go on like this for months and months?'

'You. Tell her to pull herself together and you want decent grub once more.'

'You can talk real bloody stupid! You think she'd take that from me? It's you who's got to go to her and say how terribly sorry you are that you were such a bloody fool.'

'Haven't I tried to apologize? Didn't I bring back flowers for the second time yesterday? And what about the box of Belgian chocolates that cost more than three bottles of Soberano?'

'None of that got anywhere, did it?'

'Well, there's nothing more I can do. It's up to you.'

'That's rich, that is! Whose fault was it? Yours!' In his excitement, Jaime raised his voice.

Dolores pushed her way through the bead curtain; one strand became caught over her shoulder and she swept this aside with a melodramatic gesture. 'What has my cousin been up to now?'

'He's not done anything,' Jaime mumbled.

'Then since you will have done even less, you are not in a position to complain . . . The meal is ready, but perhaps you both wish to have more time in which to drink yourselves silly so that you will find your jokes about the food even more amusing?'

'Let's eat,' Alvarez said hastily. 'We wouldn't want the meal to be overcooked when you've gone to so much trouble to make it perfect.'

'You will be able to appreciate that?' she asked with sweet venom before she returned into the kitchen.

'I'll tell you what we're going to get,' Jaime said gloomily. 'Arros brut with the rice only half cooked.'

'Or just Granada de potatoes.'

The telephone rang. Dolores reappeared. 'Are you both deaf? Or have you already drunk so much that your legs have become divorced?'

Typically, Jaime spoke without thought. 'But you always answer.'

'It is true that in the past I have been so selfless a wife that I have turned a blind eye to your laziness. However, now my eyes are wide open. No longer will I work myself to a shadow in order that you can lead a life of luxurious sloth.' She put her hands on her hips. 'So you will answer the phone.'

As Jaime came to his feet, the ringing ceased. She returned into the kitchen.

Jaime sat, poured himself another brandy. 'They say lots of women become peculiar at a certain age.'

'They all do,' Alvarez muttered.

'Why does she talk such nonsense? Have I ever behaved like she says?'

'Of course not.'

'If she wants to sit down for a while to rest, do I shout at her to get back to work?'

'Maybe that's the problem.'

The phone rang again.

163

'It won't be for me,' Jaime said. 'You answer. And quick, before she comes back and starts up again.'

Alvarez hurried through to the front room and crossed to the telephone.

'Are you Inspector Alvarez of the Cuerpo General de Policia?' the speaker asked in accented Castilian.

'That's right.'

'You're history if you don't call off the questions.' The line went dead.

He replaced the receiver. A joke? There was one cabo at the post with a sufficiently retarded sense of humour to make such a call, but what could have provoked him to do so? '. . . call off the questions,' suggested the ongoing inquiries in Bolivia concerning Algaro and how would the cabo have known about them? And could he have spoken the few words with an air of such menace when he'd silently be laughing? Then was the threat genuine? Where drugs were concerned, there was always violence; the caller had spoken in Castilian, not Mallorquin, and the accent could well have been South American . . .

He returned to the dining room.

'Was that anything?' Jaime asked.

Dolores, who was about to serve the meal, studied him with an expression he could not read. 'Nothing of any consequence,' he answered.

'From the look on your face, it was important.'

'Try concerning yourself with your own affairs and not other people's,' Dolores snapped.

For once, Alvarez was grateful for her intervention.

He dialled Palma and had to wait a couple of minutes before Salas came on the line. 'Señor, at lunchtime I received a telephone call in which the man at the other end asked if I was Inspector Alvarez, then said, "You're history if you don't call off the questions."'

'Did you ask what he meant?'

'There wasn't the chance. He rang off as soon as he'd said that.'

'It's probably a hoax.'

'But wouldn't a hoaxer have been more inventive? How would a hoaxer know we've asked for inquiries about Algaro to be made? And maybe it's not really possible to be certain from just hearing a few words, but I'm pretty sure his accent was South American.'

'You judge the threat to be genuine?'

'I think that's likely.'

'I presume you've no idea where the call came from?'

'None whatsoever.'

'If genuine, this proves that the allegation that Algaro, when working at the embassy, was concerned with drug smuggling is virtually confirmed. At the moment we cannot judge whether the call was made on the island, the Peninsula, in England, or in Bolivia, which leaves us with no guide to the scale of events . . . The art of frightening a person into a certain course of action is to increase pressure until it is believed it can no longer be resisted. You will be contacted several times. Tell Telefonica to put a tap on your office and home lines.'

'Señor, I –' Alvarez stopped.

'Well?'

'If the threat is genuine, then it will be executed . . .' He gulped. There were times when the choice of the wrong word was worse than unfortunate. 'So will we ask the inquiries to be discontinued?'

'Good God, what a ridiculous question!'

'But . . . As you said, pressure will be increased until it cannot be resisted.'

'My words were, until it is believed it can no longer be resisted. As a serving police officer, you are immune to such pressures.'

It was not something Alvarez had claimed.

'Inform me immediately of any further developments. Goodbye.'

It was very unusual for Salas to be sufficiently courteous to say goodbye. It had been written that one spoke kindly to a condemned man not to ease his passing, but to salve one's own conscience . . .

The thought that somewhere there was someone who had marked him down for death unless he did something he was unable to do, turned Alvarez into a complete coward. In his mind, he saw his image caught in the crosswires of telescopic sights . . .

He opened the bottom right-hand drawer and brought out the new bottle of Soberano. He lit a cigarette. When faced with imminent extinction, the long-term damages of excessive smoking and drinking became irrelevant.

Alvarez slept badly, suffering a succession of dreams which when he awoke he could not remember but was certain had been terrifying. He arrived down in the kitchen to be told by Dolores that he could get his own breakfast because she was going out. Then, just before she left, she remarked that if only men could be honest when they looked into a mirror, perhaps they wouldn't make such absurd fools of themselves. As he tried to find the chocolate, he wondered what that last waspish comment was supposed to mean?

The drink he made was neither hot and nor did it taste of chocolate; he couldn't find any coca, the barra was stale, and there was only a scraping of membrilla.

He left the house and walked to his car, parked along the road, and even in that short distance the heat and exercise made him sweat. He unlocked the driving door and was about to climb in when he noticed an envelope on the seat. He picked this up, initially thinking he must have dropped it the previous evening. He sat behind the wheel, examined the envelope to remind himself about it. It was unmarked and sealed. And now that he thought more coherently, he became certain he had not been carrying an envelope the previous evening. He slit it open with his thumb. Inside was a card, aimed at the tourist trade, which pictured a couple in an open-topped car that had stopped in a safari park. The man had his arms about the woman as he told her that he loved her so much he could die for her; unseen by him, coming in on his side of the car was a large and very hungry lion.

During the night, someone had unlocked the car, put the

card on the driving seat, relocked the car and left. The next twist of pressure . . .

He looked back along the road at his house. 'They' knew not only where he lived, but also which of the parked cars was his. 'They' were on the island. 'They' wanted him to know that they could kill him any time they wished. 'They' would be totally unconcerned about the consequences of whatever method of execution they chose. If Dolores, Jaime, Juan and Isabel might be swept up in the violence, so be it. He pictured a bomb's exploding in the middle of the night, the metal fragments piercing soft flesh, the collapsing roof crushing young bodies . . .

He drove through the narrow, twisting streets as if the hounds of hell were baying at the back wheels; those he passed cursed him for a thoughtless tourist. He rushed past the duty cabo, to the latter's astonishment, and up the stairs. He was panting for breath when he sat.

For once he was put straight through to the superior chief. 'I know I locked my car, I always do, but this morning there was an envelope on the driving seat with the card on it. They've been watching me and anything can happen to the family . . .'

'Pull yourself together,' Salas snapped.

The sharp order persuaded him to calm down. 'Señor, when I went to my car this morning, parked in the street, there was an unmarked envelope on the driving seat. At first, I just thought I must have dropped it the previous night when I returned home, but then I realized I couldn't have done. Inside was a tourist card which is obviously a threat.'

'Describe the card.'

He did so.

'Send that and the envelope to the laboratory for a priority examination; as you've handled it, they'll need a set of your prints for elimination purposes. Has Telefonica put a tap on both phones?'

'Yes, but –'

'Then that's all that can be done for the moment.'

'But . . .'

167

'What?'

'This has happened so soon after the phone call they must be in a hurry . . .'

'Pressure will be applied frequently and with increasing force. This is merely the beginning.'

'They want to stop us questioning Algaro, so surely . . .'

'I have a much better understanding of the psychology of this case than you.'

'Maybe. But I'm the bait, which makes things very personal. I want protection for my family and me.'

'There is every chance we shall identify and arrest the man or men concerned long before you are ever in real danger.'

'What if we don't? What if you're not quite as smart as you think yourself . . .'

'Be quiet! In the circumstances, I shall generously overlook that insolent remark. I suggest that it is time you remember that although a Mallorquin, you are also a Spaniard. A Spaniard is proud to face danger. What do you think goes through the mind of a matador as he faces the bull?'

If he'd any sense, the fervent wish that the bull would aim for the cape and not the suit of lights.

CHAPTER 24

They had finished supper – a truly Spartan meal – Isabel and Juan had left the house to play with friends, Dolores was washing up in the kitchen, and Alvarez and Jaime were watching football on the television. It was not an interesting match. Jaime said in a low voice: 'Tomas says there's a green film on late.'

'How late?' Alvarez asked.

'Midnight.'

'Are you staying up for it?'

'What d'you think she'd say if I did that?'

'More than you'd want to hear.'

'But we could tape it, if she didn't know.'

'How do we avoid that?'

'I've been thinking. Just before we go up to bed, you say there's an interesting documentary coming on.'

'At midnight?'

'All right, another football match from Russia.'

'You think she'll believe they play at three or four in the morning?'

'Why's she going to think that?'

'Go east and the time's earlier.'

'Then go west.'

'That's what we'll do if we're not careful.'

'I've never met anyone quibble like you do. You set the tape and then tomorrow, before you leave for work, you take it out of the machine and hide it.'

'So I take all the risks? If you ask me, it's better to forget the film. You know what women are – they have a sixth sense that tells 'em something's up. What would life be if she caught us at it?'

'Anything calls for a spot of courage and you can find a dozen reasons for not doing it.' Jaime stood and stamped his way out of the room.

The phone began to ring. Dolores looked through the bead curtain. 'Have you forgotten who's answering the phone?'

He went through to the front room and lifted the receiver.

'Is that the inspector?'

It was not a voice he knew. 'Yes.'

'Then suppose you tell me if you liked the card?'

It was astonishing that he had not initially realized the call might be from 'them'. Tension flashed. 'You've got to understand . . .' he began hoarsely.

The line went dead.

His hand shook as he dialled Telefonica. He asked for an identification of the number just called, and the man at the other end said someone would phone back when that had been established.

Since the caller had been a different man – his accent suggested a similar background – there were at least two of them; two men whose objective was to scare him into having the inquiries called off and when that failed, as Salas had made clear it must, to kill him. History proved there was no such thing as perfect security. Even were he surrounded by bodyguards, they could still kill him if they were clever and patient . . .

He returned to the dining room, opened the sideboard, brought out a bottle of brandy and a glass, poured out a very large drink.

Dolores stepped through the bead curtain. She came to a halt, hands on hips, her expression haughty. 'When God made Adam, He made a mistake.'

Because He had added imagination?

'That I should have a cousin who brings shame to my house!'

He drank, not daring to pass her to get some ice, morosely certain she had overheard Jaime's earlier suggestion that they should tape the green film. As if it mattered what he watched when he had so little life left! 'Where's the harm?' he demanded.

Dolores was surprised, even nonplussed by his rough reply. She quickly recovered her poise. 'Your depravity has reached such depths that you can ask?'

'It's only a bit of fun.'

'Sweet Mary, but I have been nurturing a viper in my home! A viper who can believe it is merely a bit of fun to debauch sweet youth!'

'You're talking nonsense.'

She held her head a fraction higher and her dark-brown eyes flashed icy fire. 'Nonsense? It is nonsense that time and again I have suffered the pain of watching you make such a sad fool of yourself that my whole family has been shamed?'

It was finally clear that they were talking at cross purposes. 'Are you going on like this because you think I've been having it off with a tourist?'

'Because you have been failing to do so. If you had the wits to look in a mirror, you would know that that is inevitable.'

'So that's what you were getting at this morning . . . The phone calls have not been from a woman.'

'You think I can believe that? When after you have spoken I see a man who has crumpled?'

'What you've been seeing is a man who's scared to hell.'

'Scared?'

When he saw her emotion change instantly from righteous anger to sharp concern, he vainly wished the words unsaid. 'Forget what I said.'

'Why are you scared?'

'Just forget it.'

'Can I do the impossible? Can I see one of my family in trouble and pass by? Enrique, you have to tell me. Why are you scared?'

'It's just some men.'

'Who are they?'

'I don't know.'

'Then how can they frighten you?'

'Because . . .'

'Because what?'

'It doesn't matter.'

'You are family. When you hurt, I hurt. And you tell me it does not matter? Enrique, you break my heart.'

He finally explained what had happened.

She sat. 'I need a drink.'

He poured her one and replenished his own glass.

'The superior chief must stop the inquiries so that you are safe,' she said.

'He won't. He believes justice is more important than the individual.'

'If you are hurt, how can there be justice?'

'There's the difference between theory and practice . . . I've decided there's only one thing to be done.'

'What's that?'

'I must move from here.'

'As if I had thrown you out? Never!'

'I cannot put you all at risk.'

'How could that be?'

'When they decide to kill me, they won't care if anyone else is hurt at the same time. They might decide to bomb this house.'

'Mother of God!' She drank deeply.

'If they know I'm no longer living here, then the four of you will be safe.'

'But you will be living alone, with no loving family to watch over you.'

'It'll be a small price to pay.'

'You must make the superior chief guard you.'

'He's promised I will be when he judges the time is right.'

'When *he* thinks it is right? What if these men choose another time?'

'I'm sure he'll work things out.'

'For you, has he ever done so in the past? How many men will he send to guard you?'

'A couple, maybe.'

'Can two be enough to make certain you're safe?'

'A dozen couldn't guarantee that.'

'Then he must do more.'

'There's nothing he can do since we've no idea who's making the threats.'

'Identify them.'

'As soon look for a grain of barley in a sackful of wheat. I've spoken to two different men; there may be more, but I doubt that, because too many would risk becoming conspicuous. How do you identify two out of hundreds of thousands of tourists from all corners of the globe when all that we know about them is that they may be from South America and if so, probably from Bolivia?'

'There has to be a way.'

The phone rang. When he saw Dolores's expression, he said hastily: 'That will be Telefonica telling me if they managed to trace the call.' He went through to the front room.

A woman told him: 'It was made from a public call-box in Carrer Alcina, Cala Beston.'

He returned to the dining room.

'Well?' Dolores said, her voice high.

'The call was from Cala Beston.'

'Sweet Mary, they are here; on the island!'

'They had to be, to have left the card in my car.'

'You must tell the superior chief.'

'In a minute.' He lifted his glass and drained it.

'Why do you just sit there? Tell him to send every man in the Cuerpo, every guardia, every member of the policia local, to find these murderers in Cala Beston.'

'Impossible.'

'Why?'

'He doesn't have the authority over other forces.'

'You worry about authority when they are out there, waiting to kill you?'

'I don't, but he will.'

'Then tell him he must not! Are you going to go on sitting there, doing nothing, like a rabbit caught in the headlights of a car?'

'You don't know what the situation is.'

'I understand that there are two men in Cala Beston who have to be found . . .'

'Since the call was made from there, they are hiding out somewhere else.'

'How can you be so certain?'

'That's the way they work.'

'But . . .'

'Leave it. We know what we're doing, you don't.'

She looked pityingly at him.

CHAPTER 25

Alvarez accepted his cowardice, but this did not bring the relief that confession was supposed to offer. He tried to assure himself that Salas had to be correct and the unknown men would continue to apply an ever-increasing pressure rather than wreak quick revenge for his lack of cooperation, but remembered reading that Bolivians had trigger-quick tempers . . .

For the fourth time in a quarter of an hour, he crossed the bar, on the ground floor of the hostal, and stared through the window at the people on the lower and the visible upper part of the square. Was there anyone who worked so hard at being inconspicuous that to a trained observer he became obvious . . .

He left the hostal and crossed the lower square to turn into the road which led down to the post. When halfway along, he heard the sound of rapid footsteps and swung round, arms raised to try to defend himself. A bearded tourist hurriedly stepped into the road in order to pass him at a safe distance . . .

When he reached the post, he was sweating freely.

'You look like you're just back from a six-day fiesta,' the duty cabo said, and laughed.

As soon as he was seated in his office, he phoned Palma.

'The superior chief is very busy,' said the secretary with the plum voice.

'I must speak to him. It's a matter of life and death.'

She was unimpressed. 'It will have to wait.'

'My life or death? Tell him –'

'He may be free in half an hour's time. I suggest you phone then to find out.'

During the next half-hour, Alvarez repeatedly crossed to the window and looked down at the street, searching for the inconspicuously conspicuous watcher. He phoned as the last half-minute ticked away.

'I'm very busy,' was Salas's greeting.

'Señor, have you learned anything?'

'In connection with what?'

'With me, of course,' Alvarez replied, bemused by such indifferent stupidity.

'If there had been any development, following the phone call from Cala Beston, you would have been informed.'

'Are inquiries being made at hotels and hostals?'

'Plans to carry these out are being prepared.'

'They ought to be in progress.'

'Haste is the enemy of efficiency.'

'Maybe, but it's my friend. The men are on the island, they know where I work and live, what car I drive . . .'

'Concern is understandable, panic is not.'

'If you sat where I'm sitting, you might find things were different.'

'It is a form of insolence to suggest I might ever occupy your position . . . How many more times must I assure you that I am judging the tempo of the proceedings and when the right moment arrives, all necessary steps will be taken.'

'What if your judgement proves wrong?'

'Your attitude is in danger of raising the question whether you are even less qualified to hold the position you do than has hitherto appeared to be the case.' He rang off.

If fate were even half kind, Alvarez thought, when the men came to kill him there would be the chance to explain that it was not he who had defied their demands, it had been Salas. Let the superior chief discover the strength of his character in the face of a death threat.

Frightened, bewildered, yet angrily defiant, Dolores had slept badly and by the time she got up, she had a thumping head-ache and her temper was very short. Jaime was glad to leave for work; Juan and Isabel hurried away to play with friends.

176

She sat, rested her elbows on the kitchen table and her chin on the palms of her upturned hands, stared with unfocused gaze at the tiled wall above one of the marble working surfaces. Men liked to believe they were in control of home, country, the world, but the truth was that they were incapable of controlling even themselves. Full of bombast, when directly challenged their instinct was to duck – but always with an excuse for ducking . . .

Should she travel to Palma, face the superior chief and demand he provide a regiment of bodyguards to defend Alvarez? But one had to remember that the higher a man rose in position, the more he believed in his own worth and the more he did that, the stupider he became . . .

Should she persuade Alvarez to leave the island and stay on the Peninsula so that those who wished to kill him could not find him? But when a man was thwarted, he became childishly vindictive and they might vent their feelings by killing Juan and Isabel . . .

She sighed. She would have to take matters into her own hands. Women were forever having to clear up men's mistakes.

Beatriz, a distant relation, was in her middle twenties and still single, through choice, not neglect. 'I'm sorry, but I must leave. If I'm late, the little wall-eyed rat from La Coruña causes trouble. You'd think the hotel was his, the way he goes on.'

'I need to talk, so he'll have to control himself. You work at the Hotel Monserrat in Cala Beston, don't you?' Dolores asked.

'Yes. Look, I really must go . . .'

'Are all the guests on package holidays or are some travelling independently?'

'The management tries to keep five per cent of the rooms free for casuals. Javier, the manager – very different from Alfonso – says they're so much more profitable that it's worth risking them not being occupied all the time.'

'Then ask all the staff if there are two South Americans,

perhaps from Bolivia, who are staying there. Enrique says that as they phoned from Cala Beston that's the last place they'll be, but men are so lazy that they never move a step further than they have to; if that's where they made the call, that's where they'll be.'

'I don't understand.'

'You don't need to. They'll look and act tough and make trouble just to show what great men they are.'

'I'll do what I can. Now I must leave . . .'

'How many hotels are there in Cala Beston?'

'Dozens. And then there are the hostals and self-catering flats . . .'

'Men are far too lazy to look after themselves if they can get anyone else to do the work for them, so they'll be staying in a hotel. You must know people who work in the other hotels?'

'Of course.'

'Speak to them and ask them to look out for the two South Americans and to tell their friends to do the same.'

Beatriz moved towards the door, hoping this would persuade Dolores to leave.

Dolores stayed where she was. 'One more thing. I want you to introduce me to a puta.'

'My God!' Beatriz's voice was high. 'What are you saying?'

'You will know some.'

'I will not. How could you ever think such a thing?'

'Then how about someone who makes extra pesetas from the tourists? Are you going to tell me that working in a hotel you do not know any such person?'

'That's different. It's only in the summer.'

'Name someone.'

'I don't know what she'll say if she learns I told you.'

'Nothing, when I explain why I need her help.'

'You're not telling me that Jaime –'

'This has nothing to do with Jaime,' Dolores said furiously.

Beatriz quailed before such anger. 'There's Sofia's Carolina.'

Dolores's anger changed to uncertainty. 'Are you sure? She looks so young and pure.'

'She wouldn't be very successful if she was fat and fifty, would she?'

Dolores sighed. It had become a wicked world. But then it was precisely that fact of which she intended to take advantage.

Carolina had little difficulty in attracting the attention of the two men, one older than the other, both marked by their antagonistic attitude, earlier identified as Bolivians by the porter who had carried their luggage from the taxi into the foyer and been badly tipped. They suggested drinks on the patio which overlooked the bay.

She had mastered the art of discouraging encouragement. She responded to their initial advances with sophisticated amusement, but at the same time subtly suggested that she was not really intent on rejecting their attentions; when they became more explicit, she expressed her dislike of crudeness, while intimating that she spoke from a well-bred sense of propriety, not the heart. Three-quarters of an hour after their meeting, the younger man had gained sufficient alcoholic confidence to suggest they had some real fun. She showed hesitation before remarking that the hotel was very decorously run and with little sympathy for modern amusements, so would it not be better if she drove them to her flat where no one would object to anything? The younger man said that was a great idea, but he'd drive because he never allowed himself to be driven by a woman. She replied that it was obviously time he let a woman do something unusual to him and he ceased objecting.

When they began to head inland, the older man became uneasy, for no specific reason, but responding to an instinct honed by years of living dangerously. He demanded to know where they were going and his tone scared her, but she drew courage from Dolores's words – A man will believe the moon is made of blue cheese until he gets what he wants. She told them she lived inland because there the rents were half what they were on, or very near to, the coast; the house had been turned into two flats and Veronica lived in the lower one;

Veronica was just wild and only the previous week had held a party . . .

They turned off the road on to a dirt track which led up to an old farmhouse. Just before she braked to a halt and switched off the lights, it was possible to make out the fact that the building was in a sufficient state of disrepair to be uninhabitable.

'What are you up to, you bitch?' the older man shouted as he tried to grab her before she could leave the car, but just failed. He swore violently as he wrenched open his door and jumped out, determined to run her down and beat the truth out of her. He heard a movement from behind him and began to turn, but his eyes were not adapted to the dark and he made out nothing before he was hit on the head with sufficient force to send his senses reeling. Almost as tough as he boasted, he struggled to fight back, but a second blow blasted him into unconsciousness.

Ringed by six women, Dolores held a torch so that its wide beam covered both men who were now conscious but helpless because their wrists and ankles had been secured with surgical tape, their mouths gagged with dusters, and their waists secured by cord to iron rings, once used to tether horses.

'You came here to kill my children; to blow them apart with a bomb.' Dolores's voice crackled with hatred.

Life had hardened the two men, but she really frightened them.

'I have lain in the dark and trembled at the thought of you robbing me of what I love most in this world. So now I am going to leave you in the dark to tremble, knowing that when I return, you are going to be robbed of what you, like every man, love most in this world. I will slice them off and feed them to the dogs.' Dolores swung the torch away from them and led the way out.

In the darkness, the men's imaginations reduced them to snivelling cowards.

CHAPTER 26

Alvarez lay in bed and vainly wished he had been born brave. Then he could walk the streets without imagining the blade of a knife sliding into his flesh; would not die a dozen times an hour . . .

There was a knock on the door. 'Enrique,' shouted the owner of the hostal.

'What's happened?' he replied, fearing disaster.

'You're wanted on the phone.'

'Who is it?'

'Never asked.'

No one but the family knew where he was staying. But had 'they' managed to trace him, were about to taunt him with his impotence? With trembling fingers, he pulled on trousers and shirt.

The telephone was on the half-landing and he stood by the receiver, off its stand, for several seconds before he finally found the courage to pick it up. 'Yes?' he said in a croaky voice.

'What the devil's going on?'

It was perhaps the first time that he was grateful to find his caller was the superior chief. 'In respect of what, señor?'

'Why do I have to phone your home to find out how to get hold of you? Why haven't you left a note of your new address at the post as required by regulations?'

'I decided to move away from home so that my family was no longer at risk. It then seemed better not to tell anyone at the post where I'd moved to in case someone inadvertently passed on the address.'

'It's long after eight o'clock. Why aren't you at work?'

'But it's Sunday.'

'I expect my officers to work whatever the day when there's an emergency.'

'What emergency?'

'How typical that I have to acquaint my inspector in Llueso of what has been happening in his area! . . . Last night, a little after midnight, the guardia post in Cala Beston was rung by a woman who refused to identify herself and said that two South American child killers were tied up in an old finca. Since there had been no reports of children having been murdered, or of known murderers visiting the island, the message appeared to be a hoax. However, the sarjento, a man of initiative who comes from Madrid, decided to direct a patrol car to the finca named to make certain. There, the crew discovered two men who had been bound and gagged and who were in a hysterical state. They begged to be taken away before the women returned and cut off . . .'

'Yes, señor?'

'It is immaterial. They were taken back to the post and questioned; by then recovered, they made the absurd claim that it had been a joke which had gone wrong and even went so far as to deny that they had ever said they had been attacked, tied up, and threatened by women. They were staying at the Hotel Emperatriz and the rooms they occupied were searched. Amongst their baggage were found two handguns. Their passports showed them to be Bolivian and . . .'

'Bolivian!'

'That's what I have just said.'

'They're the men who have been threatening me!'

'That seems very probable, which is why a request has gone through to the authorities in Bolivia for information concerning them.'

'They're in custody?'

'The handguns allow us to hold them.'

'Then I don't have to worry any more! I don't have to wonder if every man who approaches is set to kill me. I don't have to feel the cold steel sliding into me . . .'

'Control yourself.'

'Señor, if you knew how awful it has been for me . . .'

'I have no intention of dwelling on something which brings discredit to the force. What now concerns me is the part you have played in this incredible incident.'

'Me? How could it be anything to do with me?'

'Because the episode is so vulgar and ridiculous that I can be certain you are deeply involved.'

'I've been here, in the hostal, all night. Mateo, the owner, will tell you that we had a drink or two together and it was late at night – or perhaps early in the morning – before we parted.'

'On this island, where truth is adjustable, a man will swear to anything.'

'But you said it was women who tied up the two men . . .'

'That is what they claimed when hysterical. Once they regained their senses, they naturally denied such stupidity. Even if a Mallorquin woman took part in such an incident, which I can find just conceivable, it becomes inconceivable that she could then bring herself to utter such a disgusting threat.'

'You haven't said what that threat was.'

'Unlike you, I gain no pleasure from such perverse details.'

'Señor, if the attackers weren't women, why would the two Bolivians, however scared, have said they were, knowing that would turn them into a laughing-stock?'

'That is immaterial. What is very material is the question, what part did you play in this disgusting affair?'

'Absolutely none.'

'I find that impossible to believe and I warn you that when the truth is revealed, you will learn to your cost that justice can never be served by injustice.' The line went dead.

Alvarez replaced the receiver. He was a target no longer! He felt as if he had drunk deeply of the finest Vega Sicilia, had won El Gordo, could float on air . . .

When he stepped into the house, suitcase in one hand, he immediately caught the scent of rich, spicy cooking; when he entered the dining room, his hopes were running high.

Jaime, seated in an armchair, looked up. 'I thought you weren't coming back for a time?'

'Things have changed.' He put the suitcase down, looked at the bead curtain. 'Is she doing some proper cooking?'

'That's what I'm hoping.'

He drew in a deep breath. 'D'you think it could be Colomins amb salsa?'

Dolores stepped through the bead curtain. 'So it is you!' She embraced him and kissed him several times on both cheeks. 'I was just about to phone the hostel to tell you to come here for lunch.'

'Colomins amb salsa?'

'You'll just have to wait to find out,' she said archly. She returned to the kitchen.

Alvarez sat at the table. 'What's changed her around so suddenly?'

'How would I know? Unless it was Antonia,' Jaime replied.

'How could she have done anything?'

'It's like this. Most of yesterday, Dolores was real bitchy and I couldn't do anything right. Went for me all ends up because I hadn't cleaned the drain outside the kitchen. As I said to her, a bloke has to sit down and rest his limbs from time to time if he's not to wear out. You should have heard her reply. She –'

'Never mind all that.'

'Easy to say. But I do mind since it's me that gets worn out working.'

'When did Dolores change?'

'Yesterday evening, she said she was going out to see Antonia. I asked her who was going to do my supper and she called me so lazy I'd starve to death rather than make myself a sandwich. A sandwich for supper! Is that why one marries?'

'And she was different when she got back?'

'Which wasn't until nearly one o'clock. When she woke me up, I told her I'd been worried sick that something had happened to her and what did she think she was doing, being out so late. She didn't shout back at me. She didn't start spouting all that nonsense about being a person in her own right, whatever that means; she just apologized. Apologized! And this morning, she's been all cheerful and doing some proper cooking. Weird, that's what it is. Like I always say, if you can understand a woman, you need to have your brains tested. One moment sweet, the next sourer than a lemon in October. If us men acted like them, the world would be in a right proper mess . . .'

Alvarez ceased to listen as a frightening possibility occurred to him. Dolores's mood had changed dramatically between early evening and the middle of the night; she had left Jaime to get his own supper when normally she would never consider such a dereliction of her duties; she never stayed out late in the evenings because she needed to be at home to be certain Juan and Isabel were safe; she was not particularly friendly with Antonia; she had decided to cook a special meal before he had arrived, yet how could she have known there was cause to celebrate when he had not told her what had happened? When the two Bolivians had been found, they had hysterically claimed to have been attacked by many women . . .

If he had a word with Antonia, he might be able to learn what was the truth, but there were some truths that a sensible man made certain he never did know . . .

'So what do you think?' Jaime asked.

'That I need a drink.'

'It's still early. I mean, she sees us drinking now and maybe it'll push her back into a mood.'

'I doubt that very much.' Alvarez leaned across to open the door of the sideboard.

CHAPTER 27

Salas rang in the middle of Thursday morning. 'I have received a report from La Paz, issued under the authority of the Commandant-General of Police. Attempts to find and apprehend Algaro have failed, but it is certain that he returned to the country around the beginning of July. A minor member of the drugs combine has confirmed Algaro was engaged in drug trafficking; he also says there is a strong rumour Algaro has been eliminated because he was seen as a potential danger – there has been no sign of him around his old haunts.

'The passports of the two men arrested in Cala Beston were issued in the names of Nicolle and Chavez, but their true identities have been established as Rivera and Estrada, known criminals. Rivera has a reputation as a successful hit man. Both are wanted for questioning in Bolivia, so a request for their extradition is being prepared.

'We can, in the light of these facts, plot the course of events. While at the embassy in London, Zavala was organizing trafficking; his relationship with Algaro was not of the nature you so regrettably saw fit to surmise, but one based on the drug trade . . .'

'Algaro was on his way back from the airport with a consignment of drugs brought in by a human mule when he hit the girl and didn't dare stop in case the car was searched; then Zavala had to grant him diplomatic immunity in order to make certain he wasn't questioned by the police . . .'

'Kindly don't interrupt. Zavala had made a fortune from his nefarious trade by the time he was forced to resign from the diplomatic service and came to live on this island . . . It's unfortunate that it clearly never occurred to you that it might be germane to question where his wealth had come from.'

'So many foreigners are rich . . .'

'Algaro, resentful that Zavala had made so much more money than he, came here to try to blackmail Zavala who, no doubt, met the attempt by pointing out that Algaro must expose his own criminal actions if he went ahead. Realizing that he dare not blackmail the other, he murdered him in an act of useless revenge.

'Had you bothered to differentiate between those facts which were important and those which were not, you would have quickly established that Zavala's death was murder, not accident, and who was the murderer.'

'Señor, I don't think that that's really justified . . .'

'I have not asked for your opinion. To suppose a man will murder merely because his bills have not been paid suggests a mind which concentrates on trivialities.'

'But the Mallorquin character . . .'

'Is one that calls into question the theory that the human race is evolving. The history of this investigation is one of incompetence and wasted time.'

'But motive was important and the initial suspects did have motives for killing Señor Zavala . . .'

'Of no account, since none of them murdered him.'

'But I had to make many inquiries before that could be certain; inquiries which may appear irrelevant now, but did not then.'

'A question of judgement. Yours failed.' Salas rang off.

Alvarez sighed. A man could only do his best and if that was not good enough . . .

The sky remained cloudless and in the last week in August, when normally the first rain fell, the temperature reached forty; those doctors fortunate enough to have tourists amongst their patients began to plan two skiing holidays in the coming winter instead of the usual one.

Alvarez, very alive to the deadly perils of heat exhaustion, left the post and began to walk very slowly along the shaded side of the road.

'Hey, Machiavelli.'

He recognized the voice and stopped, turned, and waited for Lockhart to come up to where he stood.

'I went into your cop-shop to be told you'd just left. My God, it's a furnace today! . . . There's something I want to ask you.'

'Yes, señor?'

'Not here. In a bar, over a quenching drink or two. Have you any objections to the idea?'

'None that comes readily to mind.'

When halfway along the road, they met a crowd of tourists, newly disgorged from a bus, who carelessly pushed past them, at one point all but forcing Lockhart off the pavement on to the road. When the last of them had passed, he said: 'Belgians or Glaswegians; I didn't see any of them spitting so probably they were Belgians.' He resumed walking. 'When I suffer such an ill-dressed, ill-mannered, vacuous rabble, I see the destruction wrought by the age of the common man. I suppose you see potential burglars, swindlers and rapists?'

'People who have discovered the chance to enjoy life more than their parents could.'

'The reply of an unthinking idealist.'

'Señor, idealism, thoughtless or thoughtful, is surely preferable to misanthropy?'

'Preferable to whom? . . . Do you dislike me so very much?'

'Why do you ask that?'

'Because you refuse to use my Christian name. Or is this merely indicative of your complete ignorance of the finer points of the customs of a civilized society?'

'Probably. But whose society?'

'An absurd question. English society, naturally. Forged when the country was ruled by privilege and therefore supremely civilized. I will explain things to you. Ask someone to call you by your Christian name and he responds by continuing to call you by your surname (or the anonymous "senor") and you know that he regards you as completely déclassé. Dwell on the subtlety of this. Not a harsh word spoken, not a sneering comment, yet superiority and inferiority definitively established. I have asked you to call me

Theodore. You continue to address me as "señor". I can only think the worst of myself.'

'I doubt you have ever thought badly of yourself, let alone the worst.'

'How right you are! I merely make allowances for your ignorance . . . Small wonder that wherever I go, I sing the praises of a Mallorquin inspector who cannot quite camouflage his practical intelligence.'

They reached a bar in one of the side roads, only occasionally invaded by tourists. A ceiling fan provided an impression of coolness. They sat by the window and in due course a waiter came to their table.

'Have you ever drunk a John Collins?' Lockhart asked.

'No, I haven't.'

'I've tried to teach them here how to make one, but they seem to find it very difficult to understand that the appeal needs to be to the eyes as well as the tongue. Will you try one?'

'I think I would prefer a coñac.'

'A man for whom custom cannot stale.' Lockhart gave the order to the waiter, watched him leave. 'A pleasant man, but lacking emotional response. Most men do. All women respond, of course, but for the wrong reasons . . . Now, you can answer my question. Does the rumour possess truth or is it the usual expression of spiteful hope?'

'What rumour are you referring to?'

'That Guido was murdered by one of his compatriots.'

'It seems certain that that was so.'

'A pity. I was hoping it would prove to be one of the more bourgeois of the expatriates. So pleasing to see virtue tumbled. Why was he killed?'

'The motive has yet to be confirmed.'

'You expect me to believe that a man of your capabilities hasn't already confirmed everything? Was it an argument over drugs?'

'Why do you suggest that?'

The waiter returned and put glasses, already frosting, down on the table, spiked the bill, left.

Lockhart studied his glass. 'The cherry has been dropped without any regard to its relationship with the slice of orange. Why do people lack all sense of style?'

'If you had to spend your day serving drinks to people, would you retain any sense of style?'

'I sincerely hope so.'

Alvarez drank. He put the glass back on the table. 'Why do you think drugs may have been involved?'

'Guido pursued pleasure relentlessly.'

'How do you know he took drugs?'

'Would you ask a bishop where he found the inspiration for his sermon on the sins of Jezebel?'

'Why didn't you tell me he took them?'

'An even more naive question for an intelligent man to ask. One never sneaks on one's friends unless there's profit to be had from doing so. Which, in a way, I suppose, is why . . .'

'Yes?'

'You must not laugh; a confession has to be taken seriously. Having been born in a country which prides itself on justice and educated to believe that only truth should sit upon the lips, I suffer that most plebeian of burdens, a conscience. And for weeks that has been demanding I tell you something I learned by chance, even though to do so might harm a friend. Fortunately, I have learned to contain my conscience, if not to stifle it, so until your confirmation a moment ago that Guido was murdered by a compatriot, I have managed to keep my lips clenched. Now, since the information cannot be of any consequence, I can release my lips and enjoy the subtle pleasure of a conscience assuaged . . . I have a very dear friend, a Mallorquin, who lives near Cardona. He is married to someone who views our friendship with that narrow dislike which comes easily to a woman who is intelligent, but lacks a broad understanding. She works for one of the larger shoe manufacturers in Inca and frequently travels to France to sell the firm's products – she speaks French faultlessly, much to the annoyance of Parisians. Because she resents my presence, I visit my friend only when she is abroad. I was with him on the day that Guido was killed and I chanced to see something that my conscience said should be told to you, yet my heart said had to be kept secret.'

'And your heart won because had you spoken to me, I should have made inquiries and your friend's wife would almost certainly have learned that you were in her home during her absence.'

'A mean, spiteful suggestion; out of my very genuine respect for you, I'll put it down to a sudden and unavoidable attack of bile. The motive for my silence was completely honourable. Knowing that, as broad-minded as you undoubtedly are, your training has led you always to suspect the worst – too much bile – I couldn't doubt what you'd think if I'd told you I'd seen a particular car near Cardona.'

'The Baileys' green shooting brake?'

Lockhart's smooth, self-consciously amused manner suddenly changed. 'You knew it was there?'

'I learned about it some time ago.'

'How very clever of you!'

It was obvious to Alvarez that he had spoilt what was to have been a dramatic scene – noble Lockhart, proving his devotion to the bonds of Platonic friendship by finally confessing the information he had withheld because he could have brought suspicion down on an innocent friend.

'I dislike clever people.'

'I'm sorry about that.'

'No, you're not. You're laughing at me because I've suffered for nothing.'

Alvarez drained his glass. 'I must go.' He stood.

Lockhart looked up and now his tone was plaintive. 'I only did it out of kindness. I'm not the selfish prick you think me. She's kind and broad-minded enough not to judge, unlike most of the others.'

'Who are you talking about?'

Alvarez's obvious surprise provided some balm for Lockhart's damaged ego. 'You're not omniscient after all? Is disappointment or relief in order?'

'Why did you say "she"?'

'How else does one in polite society refer to women if one is sufficiently fond of dogs not to want to insult them?'

'Señora Bailey was driving the car?'

'I'm very surprised it's taken a man of your mental prowess so long to work that out.'

'How could you identify her in the dark?'

'Dark? My friend had to leave to go to the airport to fetch his wife long before then.'

Alvarez sat down.

CHAPTER 28

As Alvarez drove up the dirt track to Ca'n Liodre, he recalled the words of one of the instructors at the State Training School. 'During an investigation, note well even the slightest deviation from character and seek its cause.' Had he followed that precept; had he at the time taken greater note of and remembered, instead of dismissing as unimportant and forgetting, the half-hearted suggestion in the DC's report from England that a possible reason for Bailey's having driven on after the fatal car accident and then later returning could have been because he'd had a passenger in his car whose anonymity had had at all costs to be protected and had he accepted that in view of Bailey's character it was more likely it had been the passenger he had been trying to defend rather than himself; had he appreciated the significance of Fenella's admission that only a relatively short time had elapsed between the death of her husband and her second marriage; had he recalled her fierce defence of Bailey when the question of the fatal accident had been introduced; then he would have reached the truth much sooner.

Fenella's husband had been dying at the time of the accident and because she and Bailey were two people who held loyalty to be one of the supreme virtues – and with bitter irony, had been driven by forces they could not control into disloyalty – then at all costs her husband had had to be protected from learning about his wife's betrayal. Then this had become impossible – had Fenella been so emotionally shocked by the arrest of her lover that her guard had slipped and her husband had guessed the truth? At his trial, Bailey had lacked the image of an innocent man because his conscience named him guilty, not of the girl's death, but of being responsible for Fenella's husband's suffering the truth before he died.

When it had seemed there were three possible suspects, later to become four, he should not have sought to bring the evidence to bear on one of them. From the beginning, he should have realized that the difference in the times between the murder and the sighting of the car suggested the possibility of a fourth suspect (that was, before Algaro had become the fifth), instead of searching for reasons to explain the difference in terms which fitted the theory. And when he had learned the part Algaro had played, he should not have formed a new theory and fitted the facts to that. The old instructor would have had no hesitation in telling him he'd broken or ignored every precept by which an efficient investigation was conducted . . . But there was consolation to be found in the fact that Salas had been equally ready to accept Algaro's guilt because it seemed so reasonable to suppose him guilty and the facts could be arranged to show he must be.

Then there was the time he'd visited Ca'n Liodre and Bailey had been perfectly willing to answer questions, which one would expect him to be, but had tried to persuade his wife to leave so that she could not be questioned, which one would not expect him to do . . .

He braked to a halt by the lean-to garage.

They were sitting on the patio, in the shade of the overhead vine. When the dappled sunlight shimmered across Fenella's face as the slight breeze rippled the vine leaves, Alvarez seemed to see a touch of hardness in her face.

Bailey came across the patio to meet him. 'An official visit?'

'Yes, señor.'

They crossed to the table. Fenella smiled as she greeted him.

'The visit is official, not social,' Bailey said.

'Which doesn't prevent my making coffee and bringing out some drinks before I leave.'

'Thank you, señora,' Alvarez said, 'but please don't bother yourself. And I should prefer you to stay here.'

'I have an appointment . . .'

'I am afraid you will have to cancel it.'

Bailey's tone was hard. 'You are sounding as if this is a very official visit?'

'That is so.'

'Surely,' said Fenella, 'however official, it will proceed more comfortably if you sit?'

He sat and Bailey did the same. 'Señora, on the second of last month, Señor Zavala drowned in his swimming pool. You visited him that evening . . .'

'She did not!' Bailey said fiercely.

'Your car was seen on the road leading to the valley.'

There was a long pause. Finally, Bailey said: 'I was driving it.'

'Your wife was. She was recognized.'

'By whom?'

'Someone who knows her well. And do you not remember that you were able to prove you were here at the time of Señor Zavala's death?'

Bailey stared out across the orange grove, his expression one of bitter pain. 'You've got to understand . . . How the hell can you?'

'I am here to try.'

'You, a detective?'

'I always hope that first I am someone who knows and accepts life is uneven.'

'Uneven? Mountainous. When I met Fenella . . .' He stopped.

'Shall I tell him?' she suggested.

He shrugged his shoulders.

She spoke in a voice that only occasionally exposed her feelings. 'We went to a party, both on our own, given by mutual friends. Harry was married to Anne, I was married to James; Anne was in the middle of one of her affairs, James was already a very sick man and I'd wanted to stay at home, but he insisted that my life mustn't become as narrow as his.

'We were introduced by our hostess with the traditional inane comment that we'd enjoy each other's company because we'd so much in common. Little did she guess!

195

'Love at first sight is an overworked cliché, but that doesn't prevent its happening. We fell in love during that one evening. Harry, bewildered by a wife who betrayed him at every opportunity, didn't resist; I did. James had always tried to be a good husband and it wasn't his fault that he'd failed – it was simply that emotionally we were on different wavelengths. So when he fell ill and cancer was diagnosed, I had the awful, totally illogical feeling that in some way I was to blame. This feeling became far stronger when I met someone whom I immediately knew could give me everything I needed emotionally.

'I refused to have a physical affair for a long time, but as the bible says, "The spirit indeed is willing, but the flesh is weak." Sometimes, one is overwhelmed and if an angel appeared and pleaded, one would be deaf. But I made Harry promise that all the time James lived, we'd never do anything that could let him guess I was betraying him, even if that meant we couldn't see nearly as much of each other as we longed to do. We were so careful that not even my closest female friend, with whom I've shared so many secrets, had the slightest inkling of what was happening. Then, one evening . . .' She stopped, turned away so that Alvarez could no longer see her face.

After a pause, it was Bailey who continued. 'We were returning from a small flat I'd rented when we were harried by a Jaguar which couldn't stand my keeping within the speed limit. He flashed his headlights, then accelerated past, cut in, braked and skidded slightly, hit the girl. I saw her arching through the air – not that I knew it was a body at first – but there wasn't a thing I could do. Then, God help me, my only thought was to get Fenella away so that she couldn't be involved which would make it certain James would learn we'd been together. It's haunted me ever since and it doesn't make a bloody scrap of difference that from the medical evidence it's clear the girl couldn't have survived even if a doctor had been on the spot.' He abruptly stood. 'I need a drink. I guess we all do.' He went indoors.

'Inspector,' she said, 'Harry's very emotional even though he was brought up not to be. He used to become all twisted up mentally when we . . . we made love, because as much as he longed to do it, he couldn't stop thinking about James. Emotionally, humans can be an awful disaster area.'

'I know.'

She looked straight at him, her dark eyes searching his face. 'You've suffered your own storms, haven't you? So you can understand how it was for us, an impossible mélange of pleasure and pain.'

Bailey returned with a tray on which were four bottles, three glasses, and a bowl of ice. He poured out drinks, then sat.

She said: 'I've explained how things were with us and James. He understands.'

'Then he's lucky. Most of the time, I can't. How does one explain my running away?'

'It wasn't like that.'

'It was precisely that. And that's why I was found guilty.'

'It was because you made it seem you didn't believe what you were saying.' She turned to Alvarez. 'He wasn't blaming himself for the girl's death, but for the fact that James had learned about our relationship and was suffering the pain of that knowledge. He maybe subconsciously – I still don't know – wanted to be found guilty and to be imprisoned because his own suffering would then in part atone for James's.'

How accurately he had judged! Alvarez thought. But only long after an intelligent person would have done so.

Bailey emptied his glass, proved his mind was in turmoil when he refilled it without asking either of the other two if they'd like another drink.

'What happened when you came to this island?' Alvarez asked.

'We found true happiness,' she answered.

'But only for a time,' Bailey said bitterly. 'We'd forgotten that life's always waiting for the chance to kick one in the crutch . . . It just didn't occur to either of us to connect Guido with the Zavala who'd granted the driver of the Jaguar diplomatic immunity until he started boasting how important he'd been in the Bolivian embassy in London. When we realized who he was –'

She broke in. 'I couldn't stay there, knowing I was looking at the man who'd made certain my husband died in mental pain as well as physical; had condemned Harry to prison. We came back here. He managed to calm down, because that's the kind of person he is, but I'm not. I said that we had to go and see the bastard and force him to admit what he'd done and why, so that Harry could try to get a pardon and clear his name. Harry wouldn't; for him, the past was the past. I called him a coward, and lots of other names I wish I could forget. In the end, I told him that if he was going to sit down, I wasn't. I drove off, over the limit on emotion, not alcohol.

'When I arrived at Son Fuyell, no one answered the door, so I went round the side of the house and saw Zavala down by the pool. As I approached, he went into the poolhouse and came back out with a glass which he held up and said, "Diana is reborn out of the foam. What nectar does she crave?" He put the glass down. It was so absurd, so corny, that I just stood there, wondering if this fool really could be the man who had so callously condemned Harry to jail. He'd obviously been drinking enough to think my hesitation was a woman's subtle come-on, that I'd been so smitten by his charms earlier that day, I was hoping he'd now do me the honour of bedding me. He came forward and fondled my arm. The feel was like . . . Worse than a snake's, and God, how I hate them! I lashed out, not meaning to do anything more than push him away, but caught him on the throat. He lost his balance and fell backwards, cracked his head on the chair, rolled over into the pool.' She became silent.

'And then, señora?'

'I grabbed the skimming net and tried to keep his head above water and drag him along to the shallow end, but he was very confused and struggled with the net until he jerked it out of my hands. By the time I could get hold of it again, it was obviously too late. He'd drowned. I panicked. I rushed back here.'

'You did not try mouth-to-mouth resuscitation?'

'I've just said, I panicked.'

Alvarez turned. 'And you, señor, waited until it was dark

and drove to Son Fuyell, knowing that if he'd been discovered, your arrival wouldn't be seen to be significant, if he hadn't, you'd have the chance to remove anything that might hint your wife had been there?'

'Yes,' Bailey answered.

'You brought a glass away?'

'I thought then it wouldn't be obvious someone else had been present; it would seem he had slipped, hit his head, fallen in the pool, and drowned accidentally. And Fenella couldn't remember whether she'd touched the glass before he put it down prior to touching her; if she had, her prints would have been on it.'

'Since there were two glasses, how did you know which one to take?'

'One was clean. Fenella didn't try to hurt him when she hit him, that was a purely instinctive reaction. When he was in the pool, she tried to save him.'

'I understand.'

'What happens now?'

'The law demands I make a full report of all you both have told me and this must mean a further investigation into the death of Señor Zavala. Unfortunately, it must become known that you suffered a criminal conviction in England and prior to that that you and the señora had an affair when both of you were married to other partners. This evidence, because humans haven't learned to enjoy a god's dispassion, may so influence authority that they decide the drowning was no accident . . .'

'It was!' Bailey shouted.

'Please let me finish. Regrettably, there is always a potential for conflict between justice and the law because there is always someone for whom the law will be unjust. Justice demands that the señora is not punished for something she has not done. Yet, as I have just said, one cannot be certain that a court will discard prejudice, that a judge will possess sufficient soul to understand that the confusion in her mind explains her actions when these perhaps seem inconsistent.'

'You're saying she'll be held guilty?'

'I am saying that if there is to be justice, there must not be two injustices. You were unjustly held responsible for the girl's death in England. Señor Zavala is dead, it seems very probable that Algaro also is and therefore there is no one left to testify to the truth. Yet you have paid a heavy price. How can that price begin to be repaid except by making certain that no second injustice arises? Only four people know that the señora was on the road to Cardona Valley in the earlier part of that night. You and the señora, the eyewitness whose lips are sealed because a friendship which he values very highly rests on their being so, and me. I have already forgotten what you have been telling me.'

They stared at him, bewildered, knowing a growing hope.

Alvarez drove slowly down the dirt track. Dolores had shown – assuming it had been she who had reduced two tough Bolivian hit men to trembling wrecks – that when a woman was fighting on behalf of those she loved, there were no limits to the methods she would use. So was it not likely that it would be a similar situation when the fight concerned the past rather than the future?

Could Fenella have been telling the truth up until the moment Zavala had fallen into the pool? Then she had picked up the skimming net and used it not to try to save him, but to hold his head under the water until, too dazed by the blow to his head to struggle effectively, he had drowned? . . . He would never be certain because he did not wish to be.

He drew out on to the tarmac road, only to slow down for the corner that was narrowed where a house stuck a metre out into it. Beyond, in a field, a sow, surrounded by many piglets, rooted in the ground below a fig tree. Was there a chance that Dolores was cooking porcella for lunch?